SWEET LI JIE

ALSO BY DAVID DABYDEEN

Poetry
Slave Song
Coolie Odyssey
Turner

Fiction
The Intended
Disappearance
The Counting House
A Harlot's Progress
Our Lady of Demerara
Molly and the Muslim Stick
Johnson's Dictionary

Non-Fiction
Hogarth's Blacks
Hogarth, Walpole and Commercial Britain

DAVID DABYDEEN

SWEET LI JIE

PEEPAL TREE

First published in Great Britain in 2024
Peepal Tree Press Ltd
17 King's Avenue
Leeds LS6 1QS
England

ISBN13: 9781845235918

Supported using public funding by
ARTS COUNCIL
ENGLAND

"The British and other foreigners came. There was a sudden collapse, all we built over centuries suddenly collapsed. We are all reduced to coolies, circus performers, concubines, customers, Christians."
— Tang Yu, Court Official, after the Second Opium War, 1860

"The Negroes have left, but my lands are now lush with coolies"
— Sir John Gladstone: August 1st, 1838, letter to his son, William, later Prime Minister, on his slave estates in British Guiana

"Was there a garden or was the garden a dream?"
— Jorge Luis Borges

DEDICATION
For Ameena and Sattaur Gafoor; my mother, Veronica Prasad;
my dear friend Dr Michael Mitchell.

In memory of Sir David Harrison (d.2023) of Selwyn College
Cambridge.

ACKNOWLEDGEMENTS
Rachel Dabydeen, as always.

PART ONE

CHAPTER ONE
Wuhan Province, c 1875

"My bicycle!" Sweet Li Jie cried in the second before toppling to the ground and hitting her head. Wind whipped up dew, roadside plants sneezed, were uprooted in the sudden storm. The second stretched out; she saw her plums tossed in the air and scattering – dozens of plums, the day's succour, two yuans. Two yuans for noodles, salt, pepper, even a piece of bone with some meat clinging to it, if Butcher Shen was drunk and his knife (perfected in the battlefield) failed to scrape off every shred. Butcher Shen… Normally she would tremble when thinking of him, but not in the second which seemed to stretch into a season as she fell. Neither Butcher Shen nor the loss of fruit and the day's livelihood affected her.

"My bicycle!" she cried before falling into unconsciousness. It had been nearly a year since the bicycle had become hers, a gift from Suitor Jia Yun, whom she had spurned.

The 'Sweet' was her mother's doing, to entice her out of the despair, which was Sweet Li Jie's sickness. "The girl's head crawls with lice. They have put gu into her mind; can you rid her of the poison?" Ma Hongniang pleaded.

The village doctor, Du Fu, promised he would, in return for twenty-five yuans, paid over five months. "It will take months to purge her thoughts and bring her back to laughter," Du Fu said, holding out a ball of herbs mixed in the gallbladder of a dog. "It is not just lice, but demons. Ordinary medicine can't purge her on its own. She has to dream away demons. I will give you this special herb, boil it in salt water and give it to her at night, not to drink but to breathe in the vapours, and when the sun comes up, give her a different herb to make her daydream."

"Will you make her a child again, a sweet child? Will you take two yuans and some plums?" Ma Hongniang asked in a mournful voice. She knew Du Fu was a quack who demanded too much of the villagers – all poor except Rich-Beyond-Dreams Wang Changling, who was richer by far than Quack Du Fu. He owned the land which they tilled for a sickly living, blood-rents drawn from them week after month after year.

"I will cure her," Quack Du Fu lied.

Ma Hongniang sensed the lie. He had taken so many yuans from so many from the time he had come to the village, and most of his remedies had failed. But she could not know this for certain, since Quack Du Fu did, on occasion, bring health to the ailing, a limb healed, a stomach pacified – small acts but signs of hope which folk seized upon out of want. Quack Du Fu was better than nothing, so they gambled their yuans on his doubtful skill.

"Two yuan! Two yuan!" Quack Du Fu said, sucking his teeth, hawking and spitting on the ground just in front of Ma Hongniang's feet, at the doorway, knowing that she would not step past the phlegm, such was her superstition. Yellow phlegm. He had been careful to chew dried mango, fennel seeds and burdock before coming. Yellow as jaundice, as fever, as pus, which, if she walked over the spit, could afflict her with such diseases.

"Can you make her dream happy things, after the demons go?" Ma Hongniang asked, still wanting to believe. Her own dreams were unchanging. Many nights the broken body of her husband descended upon her, but less frequently as time passed. Sweet Li Jie had not witnessed the killing but she had heard the cries for mercy.

"I have proper herbs," Quack Du Fu assured her. Ma Hongniang paused, then gave him a coin. Maybe *her* dream was a boulder too massive to be moved, but Sweet Li Jie was a mere girl, her mind was only lightly dusted, so the demons made only faint footprints which might more easily be breathed away.

It was not lice that caused Sweet Li Jie's face to crease with worry or made her clench her mouth to prevent smiling.

"You're fifteen years of age today, and in all the time I have sought your affection, you have not once shed your sorrow,"

Suitor Jia Yun said, presenting her with his own bicycle, a rare and valuable offering, and looking upon her with deer eyes. As usual her eyes were lowered, avoiding his, and she said nothing.

"I'm going far; it will be many years before I return," he said. "Will you wait for my return? Will you run up to me as I approach with a sprig of bamboo?" Silence. A fretful look crossed her face.

Ma Hongniang, who was watching from afar, shouted to Sweet Li Jie. "Say words to comfort poor Suitor Jia Yun. Can you not see how his eyes bleed? At least give thanks for his bicycle. Pick flowers for him, a bit of fragrance clings to the hand that gives flowers."

Sweet Li Jie shuddered as Suitor Jia Yun reached out for her hand. She wanted to rise, kick away the stool, run to the barn and hide herself in the hay. Still, she let him caress her hand, stroking it as if to arouse some feeling. She remained numb within, and deaf to her mother's entreaty. She looked to the bicycle and opened her eyes wide in astonishment, and a show of gratitude.

"My burden, my curse," Ma Hongniang shouted. "To get her to smile… it's easier to cut water with a knife…" Afterwards, as she led Suitor Jia Yun out of the yard, Ma Hongniang consoled him with a hug. "She is a lonely angel inviting the night. She wants to be invisible but I will cure her before you return and I will keep her for matrimony. Come back with good health and a good fortune. Come back with glitter and sackfuls. Take this vase, it will keep her close to you."

★

In their small house made of bamboo, there was a stone bed where Sweet Li Jie slept beside her mother; two cooking pots; a water bucket; a potter's wheel; an earthen stove with corn husks for fuel; a knife, and a whetstone to sharpen it; twigs for chopsticks. A few corncobs hung drying from a roof-beam. Outside, a makeshift barn held hay for the goat and a cage for the three hens to shelter at night. Behind was a field of plum trees encircling similar houses. The field belonged to Rich-Beyond-Dreams Wang Changling. Each morning, when plum was in season, Sweet Li Jie was allowed to pick as many as she could fit into her baskets, hoist the bian dan onto her shoulder and walk the two miles to the neighbouring village to sell her stock or exchange them for onions and peppers. Her mother made pots and vases for special occasions – the Spring festival, the Pure Brightness festival, ceremonies to honour Chih-Nii and Ma-Ku, the goddesses who protected the trees from blight and the land from barrenness. The plain ones she gave away to the very poor, the widows who could not afford the expense of ceremonies. Some she painted, crushing the end of a twig and soaking it in saffron and purple from powders she ground from coloured stones harvested from the hills nearby. Three of these sold for a yuan. Plums, vases, pots, a patch of common land where villagers grew corn, milk from the goat, eggs and whatever vegetables could be harvested from their garden-plot, were all they were worth in the world.

The bicycle was a boon, multiplying their income many times over. Sweet Li Jie soon learned to steer it. She learned to balance two baskets on the handle, and one fastened behind the saddle. That way more plums could be taken to market and two trips could be made each morning. She could find space to carry a few of the smaller pots, so her mother was able to increase production. And when she returned home, there was more time to help dig the clay for her mother's pottery, scout the hills for coloured stones and prepare the kiln with freshly gathered firewood.

Ma Hongniang's purse swelled. She bought a' necklace of cinnabar beads for Sweet Li Jie, but her daughter did not care for ornaments or for her appearance. She wore the same plain dress day after day. She shunned the village girls who wove hyacinth into their hair or dyed their cheeks. Ma Hongniang despaired of her daughter's solitude. But at least Sweet Li Jie was healthy to look at, plump enough to attract suitors, especially with her long lustrous hair which made her pale skin even more translucent, with joined eyebrows adding to her value. And there was the gift of the bicycle, even though the suitor, Jia Yun, had gone away empty-handed. Ma Hongniang hoped the bicycle portended more gifts to come from other suitors. The prospect of future wealth – a porcelain washbasin perhaps, even a sewing machine – gave her comfort, so she left Sweet Li Jie to her odd ways.

Sweet Li Jie, though she showed no emotion, was grateful to be left alone. Nothing pleased her more than to wake up at first light, gather her plums and cycle to market. She grew to love the speed of the bicycle, and the skill of manoeuvring around stones and pot-holes to stay upright. The thrill of speed, of balance, and the spectacle of flowers! Before she'd had to walk, yoked to baskets of plums, so fatiguing that there was neither time nor desire to raise her eyes to the flowers that dotted the road, blooming lavender and red and purple. Now she could stop pedalling, let the bicycle flow downhill on its own and look out to the fields, to the cork oak and maple trees from which birds burst out, startled by the noise of wheels and chain. There were dozens of butterflies, fierce in colour yet so dainty at the lips of flowers, opening and closing their wings as they sipped on dew. The excitement of birds, of butterfly wings, of trees courting the wind: she would surrender to such spectacles. But though she loved the sight of these things, without warning, she would freeze. Fear made her hands tremble so she struggled to steady them on the handlebar. When she recovered, she pedalled faster, faster, to reach market and the shelter of the crowd. Her goods disposed of, she hurried to reach home, focusing on the dirt road, not daring to risk witnessing the features of the land.

When Ma Hongniang took the money Sweet Li Jie brought from the market, she noted how pale her daughter's hands were but said nothing. To question Sweet Li Jie, to seek to comfort her, would elicit no response. Best to leave her daughter to live out her torment, as she, Ma Hongniang, had done. A soldier had shattered her husband's skull, but she and her daughter had managed to escape the devils, escape through woods and over hills to this remote corner, where fruit trees were their main means of survival, but there was pasture rich enough to support a few dozen goats, and common land for corn. Sweet Li Jie was old enough to remember how they had picked their way through the woods, finding a trail here and there; wading through streams with only floating logs and tree branches to save them from drowning; inching up hills, and then down again, and when they came across a heap of dung – a leopard's or a wild boar's – taking a different direction. It was weeks before they reached the safety of the village. Wild berries and tree-bark had been their diet, but they had survived.

"What storm, what shipwreck has brought you to my house?"

Landlord Wang Changling had asked, moved by their condition. And to decreasing surprise, since he seemed to be going through some puzzling changes, he took them in readily, fed them, and provided them with new clothes. The villagers were anxious to hear about the devils who had invaded their country and were spreading in all directions. Because they were not yet near them, the villagers doubted Ma Hongniang to begin with, but when she wept a storm in telling of her husband's murder, they believed. The men who worked in the fields, instead of placing clay charms in the soil to call forth rain, planted models of soldiers. At night, they retreated to the caves in the surrounding hills, which they camouflaged with branches. Only Landlord Wang Changling stayed in his house.

He was educated. In his travels out of the village, he had learnt of rebellions against the British occupation of the northern provinces, led by the Imperial Court and its armies of kung fu warriors. He'd heard how the British put them all down, how the rebels rose up again, were quelled again. Years of uprisings, years of defeat, until the rebels dwindled to a handful of peasants wielding shovels. The British kept order. They chopped down whoever blocked their way. After a while, the Chinese did what they were told, but the peace was short-lived.

A British soldier courted a local girl with shortbread. He made a special effort to learn Mandarin. He gained her parents' consent and walked openly with her through the town. He proposed when she fell pregnant. Her parents were now of elevated status, marrying into a superior race, white men who could plough the fields with machines rather than with oxen and bare hands; who had machines that could harvest and store grain, and other machines that could rattle off bullets to clear a crowd. But many of the townsfolk resented the prospect of marriage to a foreigner. They were accustomed to soldiers looting and raping – as they themselves did in their many clan battles – but marriage was intolerable. Marriage was another form of British occupation. They caught the soldier, bled him, and fed him to the forest's wild pigs. A British contingent was dispatched to take revenge. Ma Hongniang's husband was killed, one among dozens. Order was restored.

The younger Wang Changling had respected such order. For as long as he could remember, the peasants had barely contained their hatred of him. As a child of five, they patted his head in friendly jest, especially when his parents were around, but at a safe distance they sucked their teeth and spat. He grew up listening to their complaints. Every ill – a flash flood that washed away their seeds or a hidden stone against which someone stumped his toe – was blamed on his parents. When they died, he became the landlord, the target of greater malice. He knew that the peasants had buried effigies of him at the edge of the fields, but he did not care about their superstitions. The two guns he had were sufficient to see off any attacks and for a time he had two paid spies among the peasants. No, he had not been fearful of the coming of the British. He could work with such strong people, and pay them sufficient tribute to be left alone with his kingdom of the village and its ancient fruit trees. How could such an attitude be considered disloyal? Wang Changling had grimaced at the word. Stupid! The British were only the latest conquerors, and they in turn would be hunted down with dogs. One dynasty gave way to another, warlords had come and gone, leaving behind ramparts, escarpments, walls which crumbled and were built back, only to disappear again. There was barely a field in the country which, if dug deeply enough, did not reveal generations of bones. His own family had fled from a rebellion and settled in this forgotten space where the peasants could be cowed by the odd hanging and easily kept in bonds. His father had sent a retinue of guards ahead of him, let them loose on the peasants for the week before he arrived. His father, though a warlord, was growing old and no longer cared much for the sight of blood or the screaming of victims. He was pleased that when he entered the village, all was calm. He renamed the village after himself, *The Domain of Wang Qian*. He organised the work gangs and agreed with them the terms of their bondage. He dispensed with the guards, investing instead in paid spies, so that during his reign there was little bloodshed, only a few beatings. On occasions, he provided food in addition to what the peasants reaped from the common land granted to them. This very limited generosity restrained unrest to secret cursing, hawking and spitting out of sight. The village endured; the goats multiplied; the fruit trees bloomed; the harvest of corn was regular. His father died a contented man, and his mother followed, dutifully starving herself to bring on weakness and death.

★

Wang Changling, though, had never been interested in land. When his father took him to the nearby towns whenever he travelled to buy seeds, he loved wandering in and out of the shops which sold everything from nails to candles to bundles of cloth. There was little meat, but the stalls bore small piles of fruit for those who could afford to buy. Wang tasted water chestnuts and lychees not available in his village. What aroused him more, though, were the books on sale – tattered, pages missing, but teeming with letters. His mother, seeing his interest, taught him to read and write. The daughter of a musician, she had been taught the lute. Fine-boned, delicate to the point of frailty, she seemed ideally suited to this instrument, which she played for her own contentment, but also at weddings or at harvest time. Whilst her family were not learned people, they were cultured enough to have acquired a measure of literacy. They had planned to marry her to the local schoolmaster, but Wang Changling's father forced his way into her affection. He had thugs and money at his disposal. He demanded marriage and so it came about.

When they fled their town, which had become infested with bandits, her books and lute had been left behind. In their new home, she became a ghost of herself. No more reading, no more performances for gatherings, when her fingers conjured love from the strings, arousing tears from her audience, even from her father's thugs, who laid down their staffs and blubbered shamelessly. In their new home there was mostly silence. She bathed Wang Changling. She scrubbed pots, breaking her nails. She cooked. She sewed the cloth her husband brought back from the towns. Only when Wang Changling returned one day with a package of books did she soar above her resignation to the everyday. She took care, though, not to reveal her happiness to her husband, in case he resented these scraps of freedom. For that was what the books were – a jumble of loose pages, many torn and smudged, but they bore words which drew her to the time before marriage, before she herself had become household scrap.

She taught Wang Changling every spare hour she had, but the more she brightened, the more he brooded. She sensed that he hated the land as much as she did, that he longed to be elsewhere. But nothing could be done. There could be no return to their hometown. There were waves of marauders, every ten years or so, coming from nowhere, rampaging, ruling, giving way to other gangs. And her husband was content with his new situation. Each day, he mounted his horse and went to the fields to oversee the work of his peasants. Their obedience to his every word, their flinching if he used a cruel look, gave him much pleasure. Of course, he missed the brawling of his hometown, the gang he ruled over, the joy of commandeering other men's wives, but he was older now, so he came to accept the bondage of his peasants as tribute to the ghost of an erstwhile warlord.

Such reverence in the village waned under the reign of Wang Changling. The more he travelled out of *The Domain of Wang Qian*, the more he fretted on his return. He brought back a haul of books and spent his time keeping watch over them rather than over his peasants. He read late into the night, by the light of a wicker torch and woke up fatigued and disgruntled at the prospect of having to spend a few hours in the field in a pretence of authority. The peasants could read in his frowning and fidgeting that he had lost the appetite for dominating them. Their complaints about the stubbornness of the soil grew louder. They planted only enough for their bellies. They took longer rest periods. They neglected to sharpen their tools, knowing that if they broke or rusted, Wang Changling would have to replace them. The additional cost to him was revenge for the paltry benefits they reaped from the land. One day, knowing the books had weakened Wang Changling, a group of them plotted to kill him.

Firstly, they identified his two paid spies, which was easy to do since they themselves, without adequate supervision by Wang Changling, had lowered their guard. The spies drank yellow wine and talked openly of their special bond with their master. The plotters lured them to a clump of bush at the edge of a distant field. It was a space where they murdered girls soon after they were born, feeding them dirt and stuffing their noses with pebbles. The plotters told the spies that a maiden was waiting there with a female infant. They could take her for free for the killing of the infant. The spies were both unwed men, with no experience of women. Wang Changling had demanded their sole attention until the time when he would supply them with brides. They hurried to the spot only to be beaten to death with hoe-handles and buried among the infants.

The plotters spread word that the spies had defied Wang Changling's ownership of them and run away. Wang Changling had accepted this story. But he was lonely. He retreated to town, purchased more books, and came home with Baoyu, a stunted young man, a circus performer once skilled at knife-throwing, who had fallen on hard times because he was cloudy in one eye. Wang Changling bought him cheaply. Although his aim was no longer precise, he could still throw knives into a crowd and cut a few veins. If the villagers pressed at Wang Changling's door, he could loose Baoyu on them and be sure to cause injury, however erratic. Baoyu was also deformed, half his jaw beaten soft by a previous master. Not even the neediest villager would want to marry him, so Wang Changling was assured of a lifetime's service. Best of all, Baoyu hardly slept, at the most two hours at night. He could keep guard as Wang Changling read. A bargain, Wang Changling thought, as he gave a small purse to Baoyu's master. As an added precaution, Wang Changling had heated an iron and branded Baoyu on both arms. If he ran away he could be more easily (legally) claimed when found. If Baoyu chopped off one arm, the other remained to betray him. Wang Changling was content. He read day and night, sending Baoyu into the fields to terrify the villagers. The sight of this runt on his horse, picking away at loose skin on his jaw with the tip of his knife, and then running the blade across his tongue, was enough to subdue them.

CHAPTER TWO
The Time Before – The Dreams of Wang Changling

Wang Changling, when still only shakily confident in his skill in reading and writing, had tried his hand at composing his own stories. The books he had bought were mostly about battles, and these provoked him to imitation, but at first he couldn't get beyond a sentence or two, and these were concerned with setting the scene, describing landscape, easier to write. After many trials, fist thumping of the desk, pens broken in two, inkpots shattered against the wall, and other melodramatic acts (according to Baoyu, who witnessed his master's agony from a safe distance, wondering what all the fuss was about), ideas were birthed. To begin with, Wang Changling plotted a version of himself as a foot soldier in Emperor Wu's army, grooming horses, tightening bowstrings, sharpening swords. Then, overconfident, he went to the other extreme, promoting himself to a general, his verse boasting of his bellicose appearance. He added glamour to his image. He wore a kerchief around his neck made of mulberry silk. He gave himself a certain pathos by being wounded in the arm, and being hurried off to a field hospital to be attended to by the Emperor's favourite concubine, Ying Ying. Her peach-blossomed cheeks, high forehead and dusky arched eyebrows – which, happily, were joined – captured his eyes. When she leant over him to apply plasters, he breathed in her scent of musk and orchid. He would woo her each day with a fresh bouquet of poesy composed in her honour. He was on the brink of tasting Ying Ying's lips when the jealous Emperor sent her to a distant province and ordered his execution. Wang Changling plotted his escape on the page. The night before his demise, he absconded with a trusty servant (whom he named Baoyu) to a faraway hamlet (which he named *The Domain of Wang*

Qian) and remade his life as a landlord.

Real-life Baoyu interrupted his reverie with a bowl of onion broth. "You write, you write, but you rarely eat," Baoyu chided him affectionately. "You write in sunlight, you write by wicker torch, your eyes will blur and go blind. Your neck and shoulders will become fixed in a curve. Your peasants will start laughing at you as a hunchback, instead of at me. Come, let me rub oil into your fingers to give them life."

"How are they behaving?" Wang Changling asked, dismissing Baoyu's offer.

"Badly, as usual. They know you are distracted, don't care at all about the quality of the harvest."

"Well, beat them. I pay you for such. Who have you punished today? And yesterday? And before that?"

"Only the baker, a youngster, but brazen as a bull. He is the voice of malcontent. I lash him but next day he is as surly as ever. I tell him I will chop off his fingers so he cannot massage dough, but he faces down my threat. I don't know what to do. Should I tie him up and toss him for a few hours into the cesspit? I'll prepare my knife, I will chop off one finger to start with."

Wang Changling didn't respond, too busy reading what he had written, knowing it was barely competent, no flamboyant descriptions had come from his mind. Still, he would persist. He struggled hard to continue his story, but nothing came. He chewed studiously on dried fungus and pickled bracken, hunched over his desk writing lines, then crossing them out. Night came and he was still gripping his pen as if to defend it against thieves (which he knew himself to be, having quietly stolen sentences from books, to help his story along).

He knew he had to do more reading, more preparation, for a new assault on the page. But that was exactly his predicament. All his books were about assaults, small wars and large wars, and he was growing more uneasy over all the killings, though his own father had been a (petty) warlord. Still, reading of the deeds of some of the Emperors overwhelmed him, their cruelties so stupendous that he turned page after page in disbelief, almost against his will, a slave to the act of reading. The story of Yang Lun, a rebellious peasant boy who aspired to be a prince, obsessed

Wang Changling, and strangely, for one in his position as a wealthy landowner, his sympathies were with the peasant, not with the Emperor who tortured him.

He had paused when he reached a passage about the failure of the Yang Lun Rebellion, the capture and torture of Yang Lun. He breathed in so deeply that it was as if he was suddenly released from a stranglehold. He was scared of the ability of writers to slit throats and conduct slaughter on the page. He was scared of the potential of his fancy. He called out to Baoyu for water.

"What has befallen you, master?" Baoyu asked as Wang Changling lifted the cup to his lips, hands unsteady.

"This reading, I have to foresake it," Wang Changling said. "Take these pages to the fire, rid me of them. No, rid them of me."

Baoyu would have grinned but for the condition of his jaw. "I told you so, I told you that reading and writing would be the death of you! You don't eat, you don't sleep, your eyes fret by day and by torchlight."

"Get out of my sight!" Wang Changling cried, but then relented, summoning him back. Wang Changling was fearful of being left alone in case his fancy conjured up dreadful and bloodstained scenes all on its own, and forced his hand to take up pen and create mayhem.

It was still daylight, so he had made Baoyu saddle the horses and the two of them rode to the fields to watch over the peasants. Baoyu, emboldened by his master's presence, and wanting to impress him, dismounted, took up a stone to pelt at one of the women who was resting against a tree.

"Stop your stupidness!" Wang Changling shouted, gesticulating at Baoyu, and Baoyu let the stone drop, surprised by the urgency of his master's voice. Wang Changling was surprised by his command. Normally he would have let Baoyu ill-treat the peasants with his whip. Now, such cruelty made him feel faint. He had to tighten his grip on the reins to steady both his body and his mind. Baoyu looked morosely at the stone, then looked up at his master. Wang Changling was distracted, gazing into the distance, which was within. The compassion he felt for the sleeping woman was unfamiliar. He was becoming a stranger to himself. That night he was restless, wondering what had become of him, and whether he could cure himself of his obsessive urge to read and write, which was making him in its way as disfigured as Baoyu. He resolved to become his normal self. Tomorrow and thereafter he would personally supervise Baoyu's punishment of the peasants.

Though he drank rice wine for distraction, and ate little so he would long only for food, Wang Changling still could not rid himself of the desire to read more about the Yang Lun Rebellion. He was hypnotised by the strong light of the white page before him. Baoyu had done his best to prepare more dumplings to beguile his tongue, but Wang Changling ordered him instead to shave more bamboo nibs and mix powders and liquids into ink, in preparation for his next composition. In the meantime he continued to read the fable of the Emperor and Rebel Yang Lun... a fable because its descriptions of abuse and executions were unreal, beyond belief, yet factual.

Halfway through the 'fable', Wang Changling had pledged once more to abandon books, abandon writing, abandon thoughts of merciless cruelty, abandon Concubine Ying Ying. In the following days and weeks he was too disconsolate to do anything. He stayed in bed, not bothering to wash himself or eat more than a few mouthfuls of corn. His room stank. Baoyu, devoted as ever, pleaded with him to at least trim his moustache and beard which had grown so unruly that his mouth was becoming invisible. Wang Changling took to drink instead, and, late at night, when song seized him, he had bellowed out the words his mother had taught him – childhood songs remembered scrappily, but which evoked images of his mother spooning sugared porridge into his mouth or swinging him in the air until he was dizzy with happiness. He had sought out her breast while his father snored. She gave her milk readily and when he was sated, he looked up to meet her eyes. She smiled on him and he struggled for breath because she was so beautiful. Now, he sang, between gulps of rice wine, in honour of his mother. To him his voice sounded measured, but Baoyu, sleeping on a mat by the doorway, stuffed his ears with straw to temper the noise. Wang Changling sang, imagining that his words were drifting through a meadow of poppies, gathering scent and soaring to meet the night sky where they would beguile the stars. Baoyu pressed more straws to his ears.

★

"I will be unwed all my life," Wang Changling had announced one morning as Baoyu returned from the fields. He had drunk much wine the night before and dreamed of the Emperor killing some of his concubines during the Yang Lun Rebellion. He had woken in a sweat and had this sudden thought, calling out his mother's name, remembering the lute she played, whose melody used to ease him into sleep.

"I will be unwed all my life," he told Baoyu. "My mother is not here to guide me." He paused to remember how his mother used to tell him that one day he would be blessed with a bride whom he would dote upon. His mother had said that every day he and his bride would take a leisurely walk to the river, through poppy fields, along trails sprinkled with cherry blossoms. There, under a banyan tree, shaded by its copious branches, they would spread mats on the grass, and partake of a hamper of grapes, goat cheese, and rice cakes. After they ate, his bride would play love songs on her flute. After her performance, she would unfasten her neck-lace, unthread a bead from it and present it to him. They would take a river boat to admire the willows curtseying to the water; cranes flapping to-and-fro building nests; otters digging holes in the banks. As the boat sailed on, his bride would trail her hand in the water and a tiny silver fish would leap into it and settle there, flicking now and then to catch the sunlight and still them with its beauty. She would offer the silver fish to him, a gift from the god of the river, but he would decline, kissing her hands, giving the fish back to her to gaze upon. She would stroke the body of the fish, all the while looking into his eyes, then she would place the fish back into the water, watching it pause, then dart away, leaving a bubble behind which the sun burnished in rainbow colours for a moment before it burst.

Another time, they would climb faraway hills, and when they reached the top, survey a vast meadow. Looking out at the endless grassland, Wang Changling's mind would immediately become open and forgiving.

Seasons of pleasure and laughter. Although the years would

23

come and go, the two of them would remain young and in love. The fields would prosper and the peasants would offer prayers for their health, for his bride's beauty. After the day's work, the folk would gather to sing to celebrate their good life under Wang Changling's stewardship. They would compose ditties in his honour, telling of his just and decent ways, comparing him to a rosebush, which, though it bore thorns, still breathed out such scents that even wild animals passing by stopped in awe, before fear overcame them and they ran for shelter.

That morning, he had called to Baoyu to light his pipe. He pulled on it and puffed out heavily. "My mother promised me a bride, but I will be unwed all my life," he repeated, only pride stopping his tears. Baoyu, out of respect, left the room to fetch some cherries to sweeten his master's mouth after tobacco.

On his return, an ant was running up Baoyu's neck, seeking the refuge of his beard and the remains of food. Baoyu gathered it, held it between thumb and forefinger to crush it, but Wang Changling had ordered him to stop. He made Baoyu drop the ant as he had made him drop the stone which had been intended for the sleeping woman. Wang Changling watched the ant recover, then move away, but with a limp, for Baoyu's finger had been rough. Baoyu, too, followed the ant's journey and once more grew troubled, running his tongue along his gums.

On another day, rain fell, and ants came, hundreds of them, sporting wings. Between puffs of his pipe, one flew into Wang Changling's mouth. He took it to be a sign of good luck. He blew out the tobacco smoke gently so that the ant could be ushered out without harm. Baoyu went to swat it, but once more Wang stopped his hand. He puffed again, opened his mouth and another ant was drawn in. Yes, good fortune will befall me, Wang Changling decided, allowing the ant to exit.

Ants had impressed his childhood mind. He remembered a scream and a man lying in his father's yard – why he didn't know. The man had a big lump on his head. Wang Changling's father was standing over him with a raised stick which he lowered and hid behind his back when Wang Changling approached. The man groaned and scrabbled in the dirt, trying to rise to his feet. He failed, fell again and went to sleep with his mouth open. Wang

Changling thought it was a game such as he played with other boys, chasing them with a stick to trip them up. They would tumble to the ground, roll over and pretend to be dead. Wang Changling looked up at his father, then at the stick, and beamed. His father had obviously won the game, and he was proud of him. The loser – the man on the ground with his mouth open – was a good player. He did not stir even when some ants ran up his face and entered his mouth. Wang Changling expected him to cough or spit them out, but he stayed still and the ants entered and departed at will, as if they too were part of the game.

"Put out some soup for them," Wang Changling ordered Baoyu. "Put out a bowl of wine. Let us welcome them in the season of rain. When it is time for ants to die, they get wings." Baoyu obeyed, pouring some wine in a saucer and placing it on the window-ledge. His master was undoubtedly mad. All his restless days and nights trying to write, then giving up and taking to drunken songs. Pieces of bamboo pen and horsehair lay scattered at his feet, even the odd one stuck in his beard without him noticing or caring. Even when Baoyu burned the stories, thinking that Wang Changling's spirit would soar with the flames, he remained depressed, muttering to himself about his mother, comparing her to ants.

"My mother's eyes were as black as these ants," Wang Changling had sighed. "My mother's hair was as black as these ants," he said, downing a cup and holding it out for Baoyu to refill. "And now she's dead, it is black ants which burrow into her grave to give her news of what life is like now, how her son is prospering…"

"I could have said as much," Baoyu muttered to himself. "Of course, graves crawl with ants, but they are looking for food, not giving out news. And what was so special about comparing black eyes and hair to black ants? Drink should make magic in the mind…"

"I will live by the memories of my mother," Wang Changling told him. "My mother…" Wang Changling paused, seeing Baoyu fidgeting, licking the inside of his lips as if to clear them of remnants of food. Wang Changling had never thought to inquire about Baoyu's family. Mention of the word 'mother' seemed to have agitated him.

"Speak!" Wang Changling ordered, wanting to be distracted from his failure at writing. "Tell me of *your* mother. Does she live?"

Baoyu refused to answer, occupying himself instead by lighting another pipe and then hastening from the room.

PART TWO

CHAPTER ONE
Jia Yun in the Colony of Demerara c. 1876

3rd February

Dear Sweet Li Jie, I write from Demerara, from a small town called Gladstone. Far, far away, but I have Ma Hongniang's vase to keep me company. It survived the crossing of many seas, though the images of you she painted on both sides have been badly breathed upon by the salt air, but there's not a single crack for ants to secrete themselves. I wrapped it in one of my vests to keep it close to my heart and placed it in the sturdiest corner of my trunk. My master, Yu Hao wanted me to put a bear paw in the trunk, to bring us luck and protect us in this alien place, but I was bold enough to rebuff him. I did not want an animal remnant to rest beside you. But now I am encrusted in guilt more savage than salt, for Master Yu Hao fell to cholera a few days after we left the port of Xiamen. I cried when the ship set sail, remembering you and my family, mostly you, and I have been crying ever since. I've inherited all his cash – so many banknotes – and all his goods: sets of scissors, rulers, needles, threads of a dozen colours and so many rolls of cloth that the canoe bringing me from the ship to the Demerara shore could barely contain them. And the bear paw, too – he had put it in his own trunk, with garlic, beads, prune stones, bark, smoked fish and other charms to bring us safely to the new land. They failed him, but worked for me for I am now in possession of a small fortune. Before we left, Master Yu Hao paid for a year's supply of cloth, so every month, when a ship from Xiamen arrives, my stock almost doubles. It seems I have enough to clothe the Colony, but there are many savages here who go about naked and beadless. At least we, in the olden days, in the poorest parts of Fujian province, would gather beads and make aprons to guard our privacy. In another letter, I will tell you more. For now, I only wish to confess how Master Yu Hao's spirit has wrapped itself around me like a winding sheet, which my tears bleach with salt. Remembering you only drains more from me. At times, my eyes are cloudy; sometimes I can barely see the colours of the cloth I sell.

It has been six months since I arrived in Gladstone and started selling. I have learnt the speech of the people here, which is a corrupt version of what the Scottish Reverend Muir and Master Yu Hao taught me in China. This is what they said when they beheld me pining by the river: "Chinee, wha wrang man? Why you eye red-red? You smoke opium? Birdshit fall on your face? Chinee, don't look so glum. Here, let me give you a catfish. Go home and cook it and drink rum and when you belly full, you go sleep blacker than Rawan self." (I learnt later that Rawan was a dark-skinned villain in their Hindu folktales).

Sleep does not come easily to me; thoughts of Master Yu Hao, and of you, keep me awake. I long to dream, so you can appear, but I wake up blackly. In any case, the night air is full of noises, huge moths like kites, treefrogs calling, monkeys caterwauling, the death throes of animals and the glee of their predators. The jungle is maw and saliva. In the rainy months the jungle is a mouthful of phlegm. It threatens to swallow up my shop, and the whole town. I ventured into it once. I hurried out. The jungle reminds me of home – of killings and more killings. Demerara is backward but at least there are no warlords here, only the British, and they keep good order, mostly.

★

10th February.

Dear Sweet Li Jie, today the rains came continuously and will persist for some time, according to Harris, my helper, who can read the sky and the fidgeting of animals. I stayed indoors to take stock, but could barely concentrate because of my grief on the anniversary of Master Yu Hao's death. All I am is because of him. He employed me as a shop assistant and over the years taught me the names of different threads, weaves, buttons, patterns. He was

30

so knowing of the world outside our town, since he traded with the British, buying fashionable goods from them to sell to the few Chinese who could afford such imports. So I learnt about edgings and laces, cambrick, cassimere, muslin, Malabar handkerchiefs, Dutch linen, bobbins. The British merchants gave him the latest news of Europe. I had heard of the threat of war from Reverend Muir but Master Yu Hao was more up-to-date. When rumours of war were rife, he decided to sell up, before the fires moved from Europe to engulf China. The Germans, the French and the British had already made settlements in China, Master Yu Hao told me, and the Japanese were on the prowl. Our politicians had become warlords, squabbling over the remains of the Qing Dynasty. I threw my belongings into a trunk and visited you for the last time to leave my bicycle, which was originally a most generous gift from Master Yu Hao. It was only on board that I learnt about its dark history and I've been fearful ever since that the bicycle will bring calamity to you, that you will fall from it, break your neck and be crippled all your life...

How often have I prayed that a wild boar will stray into your garden and trample over it, rendering the bicycle useless. Or in my desperation I even hoped that crops have failed, that hunger has forced Ma Hongniang to sell the bicycle, albeit for some bowls of lukewarm soup, and you and she will follow me here...

Master Yu Hao bought a large quantity of cheaper cloth and he and I set off for Demerara, as far away as possible from Fujian Province and the coming conflict. His British trader friends advised him to come here, because of plentiful gold. Of course, I was stricken with guilt for abandoning you, though you were never promised to me, apart from Ma Hongniang's half-hearted attempt to commit us to each other. I consoled myself with the thought that you were under the protection of Wang Changling and would remain safe. When you visited the market with Wang Changling, I learnt from popular gossip what a wily man he was. Folk told me he was selfish and cunning enough to make peace with the new warlords, having descended from such strata. He would be ready to pay tribute to the new warlords, like surrendering the young peasant girls to supply their needs. This would secure his place as sovereign of the village. A vile man, but in times

31

of great danger it is best to shelter with the shameless. How different he was from my patron and protector, Master Yu Hao, who was the very flesh of kindness. He and I had the finest cabin, for the British captain had once traded with Master Yu Hao and respected his honesty, which he thought was unusual for a Chinese, deeming them to be cheats and cut-throats. Master Yu Hao shared his food with the poorest, feeding them from the comfort of our own cabin. There were so many desperate folk on the ship, signed up for labour in the canefields of Demerara. He gave them bars of soap to keep themselves clean during the three months' voyage. He listened thoughtfully to their stories of the distress which made them leave their homes to travel thousands of miles away – drought, debt, expulsion from family, banditry, and now the terror of war. They were mostly men, having secreted their families in caves or with kindly relatives, planning to send for them once settled in Demerara. Master Yu Hao sought to reassure them that the British were reasonable masters, that their duties in the new land would be bearable, that after five years they could return home with their savings or stay on to make more. He told them that many Chinese had come to Demerara before them, and had settled safely in the colony, owning land, livestock, groceries and other businesses. This calmed them considerably and they looked up to Master Yu Hao as an oracle and sage.

★

It was during one such conversation with Master Yu Hao about our own prospects in Demerara that his voice suddenly dipped and he whispered to me the story of your bicycle.

A drunken British officer, the owner of the bicycle, had settled into a bar in a nearby town. The clients there treated him with respect, they gave him a comfortable chair and some liquor but he was quarrelsome. He insulted someone's wife and the man took offence and slammed his fist into his face. The officer staggered out, bleeding from the nose. Everybody scooted off in all directions but the officer shot at one of them and he bled to death. No one could come to stem the flow because the drunken officer kept firing a pistol in the air to summon help. He had heard the details from the man's widow. She was completely dependent on her husband's wages. He was a hard-working cattle herder. Their savings were spent, and only small compensation money and the bicycle was given to her by a British official to contain the situation... In the eyes of the British, the Chinese were always ready to riot; they were by nature volatile. She sold all the jewellery she owned and finally the bicycle which she had no use for.

"I should not have bought it," my master told me, "or I should have bought it and buried it in honour of her husband, but she was so piteous and half-starved that I paid an uncommonly large sum for it. There were hardly any in the country and I saw a use for it, but I was afraid to keep it in my shop in case it brought a curse on my business... It had been part of a murder and I believed the cruel spirit of its British owner would linger in its saddle, and the memory of the happening would remain to cause harm."

Master Yu Hao looked at me with stricken eyes, then stared at his feet. For the first time in my life I kowtowed to him. He pulled me up immediately, embraced me. "I paid so much for the bicycle, I did not want to waste the money, though my shop sales were booming... It was greed on my part. I should never have given you the bicycle, but buried it instead."

But, Sweet Li Jie, for me the bicycle was a boon, not a curse! I hope it will be the same for you. Master Yu Hao had taken me on as his apprentice. I lived miles from the shop. It saved me much effort to get there. Having the bicycle meant I could work longer hours and quickly learn the craft of patterning and cutting cloth. I loved ringing the bell to greet my friends along the way, stopping to hoist them onto the sidebar when they were taking bags of corn to market. What befell Master Yu Hao, though, brought doubt to me. One morning, he fell from his cabin bed onto the floor, vomiting. The sea was calm. I knew it was not a normal sickness. Cramps seized his stomach. His body leaked what looked like rice water. His skin turned bluish grey. He gripped my hand with a final mighty strength, then died. The ship's surgeon had spent five hours tending to him, but without luck. I looked on in a helpless daze.

Cholera. Such a swift and merciless end. Four of us Chinese had died before and were thrown overboard. The ship's surgeon, a young Englishman called Dr Richmond, worked day and night to contain the disease. The decks and sleeping quarters were scrubbed and sprinkled with chloride of lime to kill off germs. The ailing were saved with a diet of sago and rum he himself concocted. Dr Richmond was a man of such courage, such loyalty to his calling! He could easily have separated the sick from the well, placed them in an isolated cabin and left them to their certain death. He could have persuaded the Captain, who was being paid a bounty for each coolie landed, to press on, knowing that the disease would peter out after consuming a quarter or so of the human cargo. Or he could have ordered a speedy return to port to unload sick coolies, get new stock – in the meantime secluding himself from the disease. But no, he moved among us, dispensing food, even feeding the two children on board with his own hands, when their parents were too weakened to do so. The cholera was contained. Only six died, including Dr Richmond. I used to watch him ministering to folk with minor ailments before the cholera struck. He provided syrups and powders to relieve a cold or a sore throat; bandages and plasters for small bruises and cuts. Afterwards, he would sit in a quiet corner of the top deck, a makeshift table before him, and write in a book.

"My diary, for my mother," he said when I plucked up courage to idle beside him. "She has never travelled overseas, so I tell her all I do, all I've seen. Sea-snakes, whales, dolphins, shipwrecks… Even if I see little of note, I still write, inventing an albatross in flight and the like, things that will excite her mind." He grinned at me. "Maybe I'll put you in my diary – except you look a decent enough fellow. I'll have to befoul you so that my mother will gasp and faint, thinking that I am among cannibals!" His grin changed into a loud chuckle.

Whenever Master Yu Hao freed me from waiting on him, and on the wretched whom he took into his cabin, I would seek out Dr Richmond. He let me hold his diary and open it at any page. I could read English easily, but stumbled over foreign words. "That's Latin," he explained. "Sayings from ancient writers. Here, let me read it to you." He declaimed a sentence or two, then translated them. "Repeat what I have just said, commit the English to your memory. I will not converse with you again until you know those words by heart." I obeyed him and spent the rest of the day rehearsing the phrases.

Next day, I went to him and declaimed the words.

"You have a quick brain," he said. "Terence is the poet: '*Homo sum, humani nihil a me alienum puto*... I am human and I think nothing human is alien to me.' He was a bit ahead of his time, Terence, the African, but I love his free spirit!" He gesticulated to the open sea and sky. I nodded in partial understanding. Now, whenever I see the wretched Chinese and Indian coolie canecutters, I recall Dr Richmond's words. One day, perhaps, Terence's free spirit will be their condition.

He told me of another ancient poet, a man called Catullus. He glanced left and right in case anyone was around before leaning towards me and whispering such profanities... Later, I realised they were not ancient at all. At the time I was shocked, but I have since heard worse from the mouths of canecutters, cursing roach, rat, each other, in a native creole as hard to follow as Latin. Dr Richmond was pleased as I stepped out of his shadow, alarmed at his recital of translated portions of Catullus. He grabbed me, pulled me to him, opened the diary and pressed my eyes to the drawings. They were of women he had attended to, undressed so he could rub potions into their skin, soothing the effects of lice and ticks. There were seven women on board and Dr Richmond had sketched them all in their nakedness. Small young breasts or sagging ones; thighs flush or mangy; bellies smooth or corrugated from childbirth. I cannot, out of shame, describe what he drew of their other parts. I looked at the sketches, then at Dr Richmond, unable to respond.

"No faces. Have you noticed?" he asked. "All their identities are shielded as a proper scientist would do." He launched into a lecture on the nature of science, how surgeons had to dip their hands in blood, in beastly places, so as to survey, to learn, to cure. "Mercy is our calling. And to educate. These sketches will show what Chinese bodies look like – the women's. We know the men's since we work so many to exhaustion, but your women are hidden away; they nurture fantasies in *my* people's minds. My sketches show Chinese women to be entirely normal, my sketches will forestall the cruel acts that fantasies hatch."

In our following meetings I learnt that he was from the better sort of white people, those who spend great energy studying languages, history, science, all for the sake of learning, but in Dr Richmond's case, to equip him also with medical skills. I survived the passage from China because of him. His blessing was to sustain my life but also to make me accept my status without complaint. Just by talking to me he made me realise I could never become a surgeon, so much learning to do – so much dipping into the sewer of bodily fluids. Nor could I ever become a gentleman, my mind was not bright enough for the likes of Terence and Catullus. My calling was cloth. Let me be content.

★

Four coolie corpses hastily wrapped in sheets and thrown overboard, but when their time came, both Dr Richmond and Master Yu Hao were prepared in ceremony. The sailors were fearful of touching them though the cholera was spent, and I took it upon myself to bathe them, dress them, sprinkle scent over them, wrap them in their hammocks. To save his mother's blushes, I put Dr Richmond's diary with its indelicate sketches in his hammock with him. The captain and crew sang hymns. The captain led the prayers. He spoke of Dr Richmond as a man of aristocratic breeding, and Master Yu Hao as an honest trader and fellow Christian. In preparation for the voyage to Demerara, Master Yu Hao thought it prudent to be baptized, having been advised by an English broker that it would elevate him in the eyes of the British authorities. What use now, such advice? He was given up to sea and shark.

CHAPTER TWO
My progress in Demerara
28 February

Before leaving for Gladstone, where I now am, I spent a few weeks in the capital, Georgetown, in cheap lodgings after I disembarked. A man introduced himself to me as 'Mr Fu', a Chinese man long settled in the Colony. He rented dwellings for newcomers like me. Because of the quantity of my stock, he placed me in the largest room, charging me the highest rent. The expense bothered me but I needed to rest, to cleanse myself thoroughly of the salt wind and spume that had penetrated my skin. The house was empty. My Chinese fellow travellers had dispersed as soon as we landed, met by agents and taken to various sugar plantations. I was glad to be alone, after the weeks of forced friendships, forced conversations. I had time to myself, to grieve for Master Yu Hao and Dr Richmond, to think of you, my Sweet Li Jie, and to prepare my future.

"Why you come so far from home to this place?" Mr Fu asked, eyeing me suspiciously because he could see I had not come as a labourer to work on a sugar estate.

"Work, what else?" I replied. "I inherited this stock of cloth," I added, to assure him that I was not a runaway criminal. I had met many such on the ship who were fleeing debtors or the police. They planned to spend a few years in the Colony, then return when memory of their ill-doings had grown faint. I explained that the rest of us travelled to avoid the coming upheaval in Fujian Province. I suspected the war-news had not as yet reached Mr Fu.

"They treat Chinese people badly here," he said in a conspiratorial tone. "Why, I ask myself, after all these years we've been here? We only come to make little living, not a fortune." He went on to explain why few new Chinese came to work under contract

37

in the canefields. The managers bullied them, because they could. "If you fall sick, then it's jail for you. If you slacken at work, to catch your breath, then he'll land a shovel-blow on your head. If a manager don't like the look of you, he will work you late into the night in the factory. If you quarrel over your pay, worse still. I was told about one man, Ting," he told me. "It was before my time. Ting fought back, he stabbed a white man with a cooking knife. What they did to him I won't tell you. Afterwards, every Chinese who landed here was given the nickname Ting. Me too. I can't remember why, but one manager jeered at me, cursed me by calling me 'No Ting'. I had enough sense to kowtow to him."

According to Mr Fu, the Chinese wilted under the heat and the whip. As soon as their contracts ended, they set up some kind of selling business. Anything from matches, soap, brooms, before they moved up to owning shops and selling hardware or timber and gold. "I went into property." He looked around, forcing a smile, for he knew how shabby the room looked.

"You've done very well," I said. "Please let me give you some cloth to make new curtains." This offer softened him, as I expected, and when he refused – no, no, no, his hands a flurry of false pride – I repeated my offer, having calculated that his refusal was half-hearted, to save face.

Mr Fu cooked duck for me that first night. He seemed eager to impress me, so he could rise in my estimation. "Tomorrow or whenever you are rested, I will show you Georgetown," he said. He gathered up all the duck bones and took them to the kitchen where another heap lay in a basin. "I dry them in the sun, grind them down to dust, boil them and add gravy and pepper. A nice welcoming soup for new lodgers, twenty cents only." I could see he immediately regretted telling me this. It made him sound mean and, given the abundance of my stock of cloth, a lesser man. Of course, I pretended I didn't see the shame in his face, quickly starting a new conversation on the plight of the early Chinese coolies. Mr Fu was glad to tell me more about their maltreatment on the plantations. Surviving such abuse, and prospering, was his way of bidding for my respect.

"You are a worthy countryman," I told him before retiring to bed. "It is my good fortune to have arrived at your hotel."

★

3rd March

Mr Fu took me on a tour of Georgetown. What evidence of variety! I saw white folk dressed in calico, muslin, satin, cotton, cambric; men in frock coats, white waistcoats, even in the tropical heat; women in white, gossamer-laced stockings, with blue ribbons around their necks floating in bannerets behind, many wearing white tulle and blue silk bonnets trimmed with pink flowers. White men, lively with conversation, sat in their verandas playing cards or billiards. Through an open door of one bungalow, I glimpsed cane chairs, settees, mahogany tables laden with ornate candle sticks and hurricane lamps. A few reclined on sofas on the front porch, like pigs in a couch of grass. When the white folk looked at me, I felt poorly dressed, though I was wearing my best garments. I sweated from their gaze as much as from the sun. Mr Fu in a vest, half pants and slippers was unconcerned; he had long settled for being a nameless 'chinee', a low/no ting.

"Who cares, once you make enough money," he said as we took refuge from the heat in a small Chinese cook shop shaded by a flamboyant tree. He bit hungrily at a rack of roast ribs, calling the waiter for more dumplings, more chow mein. He ate so plentifully that he could hardly finish the dessert of four bananas in syrup, flinging one to the sow grazing at the side of the yard. "She next week! Give her time to get plump!" He stared at my hands as I counted out the dollar notes then looked up at me admiringly. "Man, you are a true countryman," he said, growing hungry again and calling for a jug of coconut water. Three prolonged belches cleared space in his stomach. Once more, I was thankful for the unexpected bounty of Master Yu Hao's dollars. I felt guilty having to spend so much on Glutton Fu (as I renamed him) when Master Yu Hao would have wanted me to provide for more needy and deserving mouths.

"For this simple meal I will give you worthy advice," he said, leaning towards me as if not wanting anyone else to hear. There was no one in the cook shop, apart from the chef who was also waiter, but Glutton Fu wanted me to think he was sharing a valuable secret. Was he about to divulge where the richest goldfield lay? What part of the river was best for diving for diamonds? On board ship, my fellow voyagers had stared at a map of Demerara one of them had brought with them, his personal treasure. Only his Hakka tribesmen were allowed to share its secrets, in return for favours. His tribesmen had little money, so he demanded they cook for him every day, delicacies like lotus root, fried celery, rice noodles and shredded pork. They had stuffed their sacks with such dried food for the long journey. The map apparently showed where the goldfields, diamonds and the coal were. I suspected it was a fabrication but Mapman grew fat over the weeks. When we landed, he waddled off the gangplank and, after being processed, disappeared into the dusk. He abandoned his tribe and, I believe, hurried to places unmarked on the map, and burped his way to the true locations of wealth.

"Heed me carefully," Glutton Fu whispered, looking around. "Go to Gladstone Town, eight hours ride. Gladstone Town is the place, I am telling you. Only six months ago, a Chinaman lodged with me as he waited to board the ship for his passage back to Wuhan Province. He showed me his purse, emptied thirty, forty, fifty black diamonds from it into my cupped hands, to impress me with the weight of his worth. I had a reputation to protect as a hotelier, otherwise I could have murdered him on the spot!" He paused, looked again at the sow in the cookshop yard, at its trotters which would make a nice soup. "He told me all the diamonds were from the stretch of river near Gladstone Town. As soon as I could raise the money, I rushed off there, bought a nice property. You can have it for a low rent."

There was an awkward silence! I was taken aback by his shameless salesmanship. Once more I remembered my dearest Master, Yu Hao, and his decent ways. My eyes grew raw. Glutton Fu was surprised by my changed mood.

"You have to stop thinking of your village back home and the folk left behind," he said, misunderstanding my sadness. "Demerara is your place for five – ten years till you can return with glitter and sackfuls. Block out everything else from your mind."

I settled the rent with him and he made all preparations for my journey to Gladstone Town, haggling with a dray cart's owner to get me a good rate, helping me load my belongings, giving me meatballs to last the eight hours. I was thankful to him but startled at the vileness with which he beat down the dray cart's owner.

"Man, Congoeman, you stupid or what?" he asked, gathering his phlegm and spitting it out loudly, just missing the black man's feet. "Your people don't know the value of money. You get none during slave days and now you loose, your pocket jingle, you smile at the sound! Quick-quick you spend all on fancy clothes to catch woman. Black is lack. Black is slack. Don't think I don't know your ways!" He cleared his throat again and spat in a show of disgust.

The dray cart's owner remained calm, dignified. He focused on fastening the bridle and securing the load with ropes. Was he hard of hearing? Why not answer back Glutton Fu's insults with a fist or even a show of a fist? Or did he only partially understand Glutton Fu, who spoke with a thick accent?

★

8th April

Why, Sweet Li Jie, why did I put my trust in Glutton Fu? He promised a well-furnished house but I found a derelict cottage with a broken cupboard, broken table, bed missing a leg, and everything leaning in homage to the floor. When darkness came, roaches emerged and kabowra flies awoke with a vengeance. The dray cart's owner took pity on me. He hurried to the nearest shop to buy tools and brooms before the light faded. The outside latrine stank, the wood looking so frail there I had to relieve myself on the earth, like an animal. We tried our best to make repairs, but the kerosene lamps were too dim. He let me share his dray cart for the night, lying on makeshift mattresses. I soon fell asleep, in spite of the mosquitoes, for the journey over potholes and sunbaked ground had been a trial.

The next day, the dray cart's owner hired two carpenters and all was mended. He stayed on for a few hours to help the carpenters, and to dig a new latrine. He brought back, too, a large pot of yams and plantains, which we ate with bread on enamel plates. No money could repay his ready kindness to a stranger like myself! Of course I rewarded him but he would not take the money offered.

"Man, Chinee, you got to learn, otherwise folk will fleece you! Pay, but only pay enough!" We had been so busy working on the house that we had had no time for conversation. Dinner was a silent affair, both of us too tired for words. It was only when he was feeding and watering the horse, preparing to leave, that we spoke more closely.

"Me name Joseph Countryman but people does hail me as Black Duck. They say I waddle when I walk!" He broke out in hearty laughter, explaining how everybody in Demerara had call-names. I felt deeply ashamed for it was only now that I was asking him his name. Were the few weeks spent in Demerara already making me coarse?

"I don't mind people's business, but permit me to ask you why you come all this way?" Black Duck said.

"Georgetown's not for me, too much rivalry from Portuguese shops." I explained how many such shops I had passed with Glutton Fu as we wandered through Georgetown. All with large painted signboards: 'De Santos Hardware', 'D'Aguiar and Sons Ltd', 'Mendoza Haberdashery.' They sold everything, many displaying cloth and beautifully stitched garments. I told him I knew I had to settle somewhere else, so why not take up Glutton Fu's offer, suspicious though I was at the time. I could always move on. Black Duck listened, then turned his face away as if to gather his thoughts.

"True-true! Putagee [creole for 'Portuguese', Glutton Fu had taught me] taking over and hold advantage over Negroes. What eye-pass! Is we clear the bush, dig trench, take lash, and now we shoeless, we wear singlet and short pants."

It was a violent outburst, Black Duck barely pausing to catch his breath. The calm, kindly man had suddenly changed. He spoke at length on his grievances against the Portuguese. I abbreviate for you, Sweet Li Jie, and list them as follows:

(1) The Portuguese, starving in Madeira, came to cut cane, but soon took over the shop business, putting black hucksters back into slave-days beggary. (2) The British paid them higher wages than Negroes or Indian coolies because their skin was nearly white so they have advantage. (3) When they got to Demerara, people said they brought diseases. Soon, a lot of folk's foot swell up with a germ called elephantiasis, bred in Madeira; plus their breath stink from always eating garlic pork. (4) They are grasping, greedy, no respect

for the Gospels, for they open their shops on Sundays even though they claim to be Catholics. (5) Every two months, a barque from Madeira sail in with potatoes, salt fish, onions , garlic, coriander, so they can stuff themselves with home-food, while "We black people land hungry-belly in slave barque." (6) And how they show off, hanging flags, buntings from their houses, liquor stores, cocoa factory, shoe factory, match factory, plenty factory. They settle in one part of Georgetown to make it a second Madeira and don't mix, and it is black folks' land they taking over. (7) They fix their weighing scales so you pay more for less.

A long silence. After this instant lesson on tribal Demerara, Black Duck looked tired, his voice once again calm. "Yeah, all these things wear out my mind, I wish, sometimes, a boat will come and take me somewhere else."

"But you are doing well here," I said to console him. I gestured to the horse and cart.

"Horse heel wear out too – age, work. Soon I will have to butcher him and sell to Mr Fu. All-you Chinee people eat all kind of flesh."

I now had more understanding of the relationship between Glutton Fu and Black Duck. The show of contempt was just that. Glutton Fu hired Black Duck on a regular basis to ferry newcomers like me, and our goods. One day horse meat would feed his tenants and be supplied to cook-shops, the sale proceeds put down as a deposit for a new horse.

"But Chinese own lots of shops, too. Why you pick on the Portuguese?" I asked.

"They show off and stingy bad! You-all Chinee walk barefoot like we. I mean you-all are humble, 'barefoot' in mind. Chinee give we trust, too, and when Easter and Christmas come you can be sure of plenty dumpling. When baby born and you take it to the Chinee shop, they make a fuss of it, hand out free flour, cross the palm with coin. Chinee shops safe. We only raid and burn down Putagee Fernandes, Da Costa and dem."

However, this confession of racial violence unsettled him and he hastened to add: "I born Christian, I don't take part in the burning. Looting not for the likes of me. But I still feel for my fellow Negroes."

I learned quickly how you must give-and-take with the Demerara people, especially black folk ('Congoes' they are called), not long freed from slavery. When you are born in dirt and you get treated like dirt, then getting respect is more boon than bread, and if you don't give respect, then is trouble.

★

30 April
Dear Sweet Li Jie, I am safe and settling in well and making good money. I will return to you as soon as I am finished in my business. It was very different to begin with. I heard of the recent murder of a Chinese in a small settlement up the Demerara river. This was a few months before Prospect Town settlement – which I will tell you about – was established. Apparently a dozen or so Chinese had ganged together and bought land to start a new village, which they named after their village back home. They didn't intend to cultivate the land but to use it as a base for venturing deep into the jungle to prospect for gold. Folklore has it that the streams are awash with gold and the whole country was once called El Dorado for this reason. But they needed to clear bush and dig drainage to stop flooding. Clearing the bush was easy, they just set it on fire. Digging canals was impossible. Chinese men are not sturdy enough. It was a job made for Black folk. Two hundred years of slave work has turned them into brawn. I myself have seen the marvel of a Congoe man. In blazing sun, up to his hips in water, wrenching shovelful after shovelful of dense clay, then tossing these twelve or more feet clear on each side – delivered straight from his hip at the end of a six-foot shovel stick. You can stand and watch him work for hours and soon the ditch done.

A week's work for a Chinese is done by a Congoe in one day. So they handed out the job to six Congoes for three weeks. The Congoes set to work with their shovels. They love digging and they love roast pork, and the Chinese worried for the size of their swine herd. By the time the work was done, the Chinese were down two dozen prized animals!

The rains came; it slowed down progress, but the Congoes persisted as best they could. The rain was so heavy there were many days they just couldn't dig and had to stay in their makeshift

44

hut, waiting on the sun to suck up the water. The Chinese still had to feed pork to the Congoes but were getting nothing in return. They sulked, offered chicken instead, or fish, but no, once the Congoes had tasted Chinese roast pork, you couldn't pay them with chicken or fish.

At last, the ditches were ready. But the rain meant that it took the Congoes four weeks instead of the three contracted. The Congoes rightly held out for extra money. They were not to blame for the idle days. The Chinese refused. They waved their cooking knives. Then one of the Congoes put a lash on a Chinaman's head, the shovel splitting his skull.

The end was quick. The Congoes ran away into the jungle knowing that the police would blame them, for they were black. The Chinese buried their countryman, took to their barges with their remaining pigs and went back to where they started.

Glutton Fu told me this story. I don't know how true it is or whether he was just trying to frighten me as a newcomer, so I would depend on him.

★

10th May
Dear Sweet Li Jie, today I took up a cutlass and cleared nettles which have been marching towards my shop door like drunken soldiery. As soon as I cut their stems, ants appeared from nowhere to wallow in the green juice that leaked out. So I took up a spade and heaped dirt to bury them. Buried alive... I cannot escape our Chinese customs. I think of all the ruined palaces in Xiamen, each built in the footprint and shell of an earlier one... So many centuries, so many heaps of concubines not even stunned or made drunk before being thrown into their Masters' graves. Demerara makes me remember these ceremonies; the jungle fouls my mind, though I strive to think only of you. Still, the ants have to be buried alive or they would overrun my shop.

I planned to employ a servant or an assistant but I could find no trusted Chinese, so I took on a light-skinned Negro, a man called Harris. There are hundreds upon hundreds of Chinese here, but most are more interested in getting gold from the sides of streams and rivers than building up a business over years. For me, bind your belly, patience, purpose – only these will do. I measure and price my cloth carefully – not too much profit, not too little. I take stock at the end of each day, put aside two or three leftover pieces for the poor. I count my takings, bury most in a jar as savings, which I will exchange for gold to fetch you. The rest will keep me in food and lamp oil. But I must not bore you with my business, except to tell you about how I sell to the poor. They're mostly Indian coolies outside Gladstone Town. It's too far for them to walk to my shop which I set up in the front yard. It's a hut more than a proper shop, but secure from the weather. So I go out to them. I move in a donkey cart with Harris, loaded up with sufficient cloth, not too much for the sun will bleach the colours, not too much because I want the buyers to beg me to return. Donkey and me and Harris go to villages with grand British names – Trafalgar, Brighton, Victoria – names which don't at all match the jumble of mud-and-wattle huts held up by manicole palm stems, spiked or sagging troolie-leaf roofs which look as they've been shaved by a drunken barber. I find a shady tree, stop. Harris rings a bell or blows a conch, and the people run out, as if I had kicked over an ants-nest. I have a large bucket of water. Before they can feel the cloth they must first wash their hands. Harris pours out the water. Before they start haggling (or rather cursing me), to dampen their passion, I call to the skinniest woman in the crowd.

"Wha your name?" I ask.

"Me name Pakul," she answers.

"Pakul, you get child-pickni?"

"Beta, me make ten but three dead out."

Oh, how I love the sound of these Hindi greetings, beta, bhai, chacha, mamu!

"Sorry-sorry," I tell her. (At this point the crowd is stilled, remembering their own losses.)

"The rest of them get work?" I ask in a trembling voice.

"Dem plant garden. Why you ask?"

"Because me want give you this piece a cloth free." I hold up a length for all to behold, then, as if on second thoughts, I hold up another. "Take all two, clothe your pickni." At this point she grabs the cloth and starts running away in case I change my mind and was mocking her. Then, she stops and turns around, remember-

46

ing her Hindu duty to give thanks.

"Wait ya, me go give you some strings bora. Chineee does eat bora or is pumpkin you want?"

I decline, bowing to her with respect.

"Keep food for your pickni (creole for 'child'), me belly full."

I pull up my vest, swell out my belly and rub it to provoke merriment. The time is now ripe to start the selling. I hold up lengths of yellow and green cloth (coolies prefer these colours, the brighter the better), carefully cut and measured in my shop beforehand so all sizes of women could be catered for. I always have pieces of chiffon for their headdresses. The Hindu houses bear red and white prayer flags waggling from bamboo poles. I make sure I have an ample supply of cloth to make these, again cut to the inch. Here, the people have a saying, 'one-one dutty mek dam', meaning each piece of earth, however small, put together will make a dam. In my business it is the one-one inch makes five yards and $7 profit, which can buy one pennyweight gold which I can resell for $8. From one full moon to the next, the money heaps up, and I start over again and again, until one day, I can have enough 'dutty' to build a dam across the ocean to greet you, Sweet Li Jie. But I dream… I will, for certain, have enough to hire a ship-cabin, spacious and cushioned and furnished with all conveniences, so that when you land in Demerara, you will be as fresh as when you left China. Many afternoons when my work is done I go to the docks to pass time, but really to stare out to the horizon and imagine your coming. I see shiploads of new arrivals, mostly from India, and when their feet touch land, they totter or hold on to each other. I look into faces flaked with salt, dry sweat, helplessness in their eyes, half naked men and women in stained clothing. No, you will be fresh and fragrant and slippered in lace when you land.

But I stray, dear Sweet Li Jie, let me tell you about the crowd around my cart. Many of them pay me right away in cash, but others demand trust.

"Man, Chinee, man, me broke, me husband drink out all de money, give me trust till month-end."

The pleas are plenty, most are ordinary: the rum-addicted husband, or the husband accidentally chopped, drained of blood and unable to work, laid up in bed, "till month end". (Always 'till month end', as if the beginning of the new month heralds a miracle). Other pleas are worthy of the finest storyteller: a lizard had fallen invisibly in her curry pot and so transformed the family that her husband's skin began to turn green and scaly. In a strong wind the scales had dislodged, floated into her neighbour's yard, and settled on the fruit trees, and all the papayas and guavas suddenly soured, so when her neighbour's goats ate the fruit that fell, they get sick, their droppings turn watery, and their goat-bubbies dry up, no milk. And because the goats were the main source of income from milk and selling the goat droppings for manure – or mixing with mud and cow dung to daub the bottom house, making a hard crust of the earth so rainwater drained away and mosquitoes couldn't breed, and the children could rock in a hammock without muddy feet – the neighbour had to be compensated. Hence no money 'till month end' when the goats were bound to heal. This woman said she had to summon the Pandit, the Hindu priest, to pray, blow a conch, sprinkle dye on the floor, and foretell that her husband and the neighbour's goats would be protected by a god named Vishnu. Apparently Vishnu is the god who has special healing powers over goats and humans who are threatening to turn into turtles or lizards or any other green and scaly creature. The Hindu gods themselves (I learnt this from Gurr – I will write about him later) are full of madness. One day a god is a cow, the next a snake. They shift shapes, they are as slippery as the 'month-end' villagers. According to Gurr, the Hindu holy books are full of stories changing into other stories and shuffling into hundreds more stories, then winding back to the beginning, then setting off again in different directions. Mayhem. It is as if I were to unspool all my threads, mix up the colours, twine them without reason, then unpick my work, neaten and order and wind them back into separate bobbins. Then the next day and the next I start unravelling and restoring again.

★

Month-end never comes, in truth, but 'month-end' is why folk stay in Demerara, though mosquito, polio, yellow fever, rabies, flood and drought are endemic.

"Why the British settle here is sheer madness!" Harris said, relaxing the reins and letting the donkey make its own way to my house. "They slave the black people from Africa to make plantation and now they harvest coolie from India for the same. Chinee too weak for the work. The British give up on them. Coolie can get free passage home when five year contract expire, but most of them stay. Why? They dream of gold like everybody else. Every few years there is a rush to the jungle, rumours of how so and so find gold, but in truth the only glow in their face is from jaundice. His pockets get a few yellow grains, that is all. 'Month-end' is the time to come, when people will find gold aplenty. Until then, they mind cow, cut cane, catch fish and beg for trust from Chinee like you." Harris shook his head, cleared his throat as if to spit, but changed his mind. It would be unlike him to spit. In the months in my employ he never showed he held anyone in contempt.

"Folk like Gurr think of themselves as small people. That is what he tell you," Harris continued. "If they reckon rightly, they would come to see they are part of a huge business which would falter without them. Africa, India, China, Britain – who would imagine that sugarcane would bind three continents. The British imagined it, so they deserve praise – but also a slap in the face! When the first British man was dreaming of sugarcane in Demerara and plotting his fortune, if only someone had come along and put one slap on him to wake him up. Wake him up to the mosquito, polio, yellow fever, rabies, flood and drought." Harris threw back his head and laughed. "They say babies born with their hands curled, but when I emerged I had my right hand open. Maybe God put me on earth to make the slap." Again, his words bore no resemblance to his character. He was more teacher than rebel. It was through his eyes that I began to glimpse the history of Demerara. But for all his evaluation of folk partaking in a master plan and striding with purpose, I only saw barebacked coolies bent before cane. And for such homage, what a stingy purse! When I idled at the dockside, imagining your coming, I would see a coolie ship offloading a few hundred men and a handful of women. Some of them were excited, the sky was loud with bird-call and the land stretched green before them. Others looked lost. Humans or rags – sometimes it was hard to tell. Unlike me, they came without cloth. What ruin drove them so far-far from their village? Some were excited to begin with, to have reached shore safely. They sniffed the air to catch the scent of the new land, and every bird flying overhead seemed to brighten their faces. The canefields will cage these coolies for five long years.

★

When the coolies talk of their plight, I think of my own. I remember you and Ma Hongniang in a wagon, Baoyu chupsing the horse, Wang Changling sitting at the back on his own, studying the titles of the books he just bought from the market. Every month the cart would come, bearing all of you, come to buy cured meat, dried fish, books. I would peep at you from behind rolls of cloth. My Master's store was at the end of the market. I always wished you could venture my way, but you'd be dawdling at Baoyu's side, hiding from the throng of shoppers. Baoyu sensed your shyness, drew you close to him and took you to the store where Wang Changling had already settled, waiting to inspect the books presented to him. The bookseller made tea for Wang Changling and gave you a stool to squat beside him. The place was always quiet. Only a few drifted in to look at books. You, your mother and Wang Changling were mostly alone, with Baoyu standing guard at the doorway. The bookseller fawned over you, knowing you were Wang Changling's favourite. He was a regular and lavish customer, so you were the beneficiary of juices and cake.

"Take your time. The day has just begun. Drink. Eat," the bookseller would say, pouring more for Wang Changling and reaching in his lunch bag for a ripe orange, peeling it delicately in spite of his fat fingers and offering it to you with an exaggerated bow. He went to pat your head but you swerved away. I wanted to wander over, to pretend I was curious about books, but really just to see you close up. I imagine you smelling of musk and orchid. I could never do this; our store was very popular, swarming with mothers in quest of bargains, displaying their urchins to me so I would take pity and reduce prices. A secret pinch here, a jook there, and the child held up to my gaze would start hollering, and Master Yu Hao would leave off his duties and rush to comfort him. Always a boy, because the mothers knew full well that

50

Master Yu Hao was single and childless; that his wife left him for an English missionary; that Master Yu Hao was therefore shunned by all women as being cursed by the gods; that he would never have a male heir to take over his business and make it prosper.

It was always a boy and Master Yu Hao would hold him close, patting his back to comfort him, to stop his slobbering. Of course, the cunning of the mothers paid off. Master Yu Hao would sell them cloth at cost price. In his mind Master Yu Hao had a host of stepchildren. A piece of fabric here, a vest there, would not bankrupt him. Indeed, with such a sense of responsibility for other people's sons, he felt he should work hard to increase profit so that more could be given.

Mothers haggling, children crying, my Master hurrying to comfort them, every day was chaos; there was hardly time to peep at you. Then Ma Hongniang came. I looked up from a heap of bales and there she was, startling me by her appearance.

"I see you staring at her," she said, nodding in your direction. "She's too young for you." We both stared at you, Sweet Li Jie, as you squatted quietly on a stool, eating the bookseller's oranges. I went to mumble something but Ma Hongniang stopped me. "Too young," she repeated. "She is fifteen, but is gowned in worry which makes her look older."

"Let me give her something bright," I blurted out, looking around at the stock. Ma Hongniang beheld me with pity.

"Wang Changling is good to her. He buys her cloth with shining patterns, sunflowers, roses. You'd think she was a meadow, but no, the dresses cannot lift the mist of gloom; it clings to her." Ma sighed and it was my turn to pity her.

"My mother and father were like that," I offered. "They are healed now."

"Your parents? Poor things, but I am glad to know they are normal again. What was the cause of their worry?"

"Oh, everything. I was a boy, maybe Sweet Li Jie's age. They were always busy, my father grazing oxen, my mother grinding corn. They cultivated a vegetable garden, always weeding, watering, setting up bamboo poles to support the plants or traps for the field mice." I paused, feeling foolish over such a disclosure of my parents' lives.

"No, no, go on, " Ma Hongniang urged. "Your stall is not busy. I waited until all were gone before coming over."

Robbed of such excuse I was obliged to continue.

"Maybe it was rumours about a coming war or invasion, I can't remember. I used to go to school – some missionaries had come to our village and set one up. They taught me to read and write English. My parents were happy. The pastor, Reverend Muir, who ran the school was a foreigner. He told us about a country or an island called Scotland. He told us about a world outside our village which was full of war. Many nations, many armies. Our own country was being drawn into a fight, a big fight which would engulf half the world. He said it was foretold in their holy books and he read out of passages from the Bible about slaughter and the fields burning and the sea turning red. 'It will be the first world war,' he said. As he spoke, he stroked his moustache, stiff, curled, from which you could hang lanterns. That night I couldn't sleep easily for fear of the weapons he described – machines made of iron which roamed the earth belching fire, or balloons dropping bombs from the air. I had a nightmare: I was lying face down in the mud, my pants blown off by cannon-fire, and the wind, knife-sharp, slicing skin from my buttocks. The next day I wouldn't go to school. I told my parents what Reverend Muir said. They, too, fell into silence."

I stopped. I would say no more to Ma Hongniang. I looked out to you again, Sweet Li Jie, eating your oranges so innocently. So innocent of the blood-letting to come. Ma Hongniang did not persist. She looked around at the bales of cloth to distract herself. A mother and son came to the store, and I moved away to serve them. When I was done, I turned to Ma Hongniang but she was gone. You too. The bookseller was smiling as he rearranged his shelves. He was pleased with his sales to Wang Changling. Master Yu Hao and I sat down to reckon our day's takings. My gloom lifted. Writing down the numbers in our ledger, subtracting and adding, forecasting the next day's profit or loss, calmed me. It is an act I've spent all my life practising, and numbers have rarely failed to pacify me.

PART THREE

CHAPTER ONE
More Time Before: Baoyu, Swallow Tail and Buttocks

"Speak! Tell me of *your* mother. Does she live?"

This was a question Baoyu would not answer even for himself. He rubbed his jaw as he remembered lying in bed in a comatose state. He was a boy of fourteen or thereabouts, the star knife-thrower in a touring circus. One night, after a performance of special quality – Baoyu dissecting one melon, then another, and smaller fruit, then, as a finale, throwing his knives between the circus master's daughter's outspread legs, evoking anxious cries from the crowd, then applause afterwards – he retired to sleep. Making his way out of the circus ring, a grateful villager thrust a gourd into his hand. It was filled with a local brew. Baoyu took a sip, swallowed, then convulsed in a fit of coughing, for he had never drunk liquor before. Still, he sipped again, and the liquor tasted better. Before too long the gourd was half-emptied and he lay in bed in his wagon enjoying the way his mind swirled and his eyes saw curious things, far more enchanting than what daily life offered. A terrapin with azure specks on its shell was inching its way up the wall of the wagon. Before it reached the top, it turned its head to Baoyu, breathed in and blew out bubbles, which the sun burnished in rainbow colours before they burst. A moth arose from a crevice in the moon, hovered over Baoyu's head, then winged its way back to its moon-shelter. A mouse ran up to him, bared its teeth, which were all of the brightest gold. The pageant of creatures continued all night. His own circus was a dismal show in comparison. The next evening his performance was perfect, but his mind didn't sparkle as before. He sought out the gourd's remaining liquor and lay in bed awaiting visions. Nothing came though, not the tiniest of mice, the most meagre of beetles.

He was so distraught that the next night his throwing was awry. He split the melon but not in an exact half. He barely sliced the orange and nearly missed the lime. When it came to the circus master's daughter, a blade seemed to brush one leg before embedding itself in the wooden board behind her. Blood appeared on the daughter's thigh, albeit only a little, but enough to make the spectators gasp and the daughter to collapse in a faint. Greater applause followed, the spectators thinking that the throw was planned.

The circus master beat him, breaking his jaw. "You scared her," he screamed. "You brought on her menses. You have made her a woman before her time." He knew this was a lie, for Swallow Tail (her circus name) at seventeen had already flowered. "You have cost me money I cannot afford, I will have to marry her off and find gold for a husband." Each accusation was accompanied by a blow, the last of which damaged one of Baoyu's eyes.

He crawled away to the nearby woods to die. It was Swallow Tail who, following the trail of blood from Baoyu's wagon, found him semiconscious on a bed of moss. She spread a cloth over him, and propped up an old blanket with sticks to serve as a tent. She washed the blood and dirt from his eye socket and mouth, rubbing oil over them to aid healing. She fed him fruit from her own hand, mashed into a pulp to help him swallow it. Best of all she give him liquor to ease his pain and bring on sleep.

No fabulous creatures came to embellish his dreams. Each night, for a week, only his mother darkened them. "I am your mother," she had to tell him, for he did not know who she was. She had sold him to the circus when he was barely seven, for ten yuans, throwing herself into the bargain by yielding her body to the circus master. "Here, I can prove I am your mother," she said, showing the stripes on her naked back. The circus master, used to whipping animals into submission so they could be trained to entertain, had done the same to her. He had taken her to a nearby cave and lashed her throughout hours of copulation.

Afterwards, when the ten yuans had been handed over, Baoyu was put into a wagon, sharing it with caged dogs that had been taught to stand on two legs and box each other. The circus moved on to a new village.

Baoyu doubted that the woman in his dream was his mother, and he discounted her tale of abuse, accusing her of exposing her scars to solicit money from him, as did the countless beggars he had met on his journeys through the province. They would rush up to greet the circus, showing off their stumps, their scars, their flesh colonised by flies. They begged for a portion of the food fed to the circus animals. The circus master cursed them and whipped them away.

"You're not my mother," Baoyu scolded her. "For a start you are tall and slender, and I am a stump of flesh. How could you have bred someone like me?"

"We were hungry beyond words when you were made," she said. "The crops failed, no rain fell, the ground was as hard as a turtle's shell. We dug up worms, but they were dying in the dry earth. There was no flesh left for us. We ate whatever leaves remained on the trees. We ate tree bark, chewed roots for a little water. Your father found a trove of coal. We ate lumps of coal to fill our stomachs – the taste so strange and delicious. I have not had such a feast since! One night, your father, fired up by the coal, found the strength to mount me one last time. Then he stumbled off into the darkness. Some wolf must have gotten him. You were born stunted, nearly spineless, weighing no more than a dry coconut. I had no milk to give, even when the rains came and corn returned. You could hardly crawl, hardly walk, so when the circus came, I sold you. I wept to see you go but I wanted you to have food. The circus had mules, horses, dogs, a dozen animals. In a season of drought at least some could be slaughtered and cooked."

Baoyu woke from his dream to find his face wet with tears and his head cradled in female arms. "Get away from me, you imposter," he cried, struggling to escape.

"Hush, hush, it's me, Swallow Tail." Baoyu looked up and saw it was not his mother. Swallow Tail embraced him and he willingly sucked broth from a spoon she fed him with. It had been a week of feeding him and washing his wounds. Baoyu, apart from his damaged eye and jaw, was returning to his normal self.

"But how can I depart from you?" he asked Swallow Tail, taking her hand, kissing it softly. "We've always been kin, though not by blood…"

"Blood brought us together," Swallow Tail said. "Don't you remember what my father did to your mother in the cave or were you too busy chasing grasshoppers? And all those beggars whose flesh he opened up with his whip? I hate my father. I am glad my mother died giving birth to me." Swallow Tail broke into tears.

Baoyu gathered her tears in the palm of his hand and salted his lips with them. "Salt will preserve our bond, always, wherever we go, however far," he said. He rubbed the rest of her tears around his eyes, to better see their future. It had been eight years since he was sold by his mother and bundled into the circus wagon. Swallow Tail, two years older than him, was living in her father's caravan. The only children in the troupe, they had sought out each other's company. In the daytime, they chased butterflies or gathered beetles in a bottle, enraptured by the way they climbed over each other, sliding off each others' backs, as they sought to escape. The butterflies were never harmed and the beetles, one by one, placed back on the ground. Swallow Tail was as soft as her name. Once, when they had heaped up dried leaves into a den and hid, pretending to be soldiers on a secret mission or robbers escaping with their haul of twigs and pebbles, Swallow Tail suddenly blurted out her hatred of her father.

"He howls when he remembers my mother," she said. "He curses her for leaving him for other men in the faraway land of the afterlife. He thumps the side of the caravan until his knuckles are sore. I hide under the blanket watching him take up a piece of rope, twisting it this way and that, making one knot, then another, as if he was intent on choking my mother. Sometimes he hurries out of the caravan and takes a whip to the animals, blaming them for poor performance, threatening to starve them to death, when all the time it was my mother he is speaking to…"

As they grew up together, Baoyu began to understand Swallow Tail's attitude to her father. She had witnessed how he seized village women, slept coarsely with them, their husbands within earshot of the whip, but in need of the coins their wives were earning. When he returned to the caravan he would scowl at Swallow Tail, for she resembled her mother who had died at childbirth to spite him, to punish him for all his wrongdoings with starving village women. Yet Swallow Tail was his only child

58

and he protected her from the gaze of other men. Only Baoyu, ugly, hunched, was allowed to play with her, otherwise she was cloistered in the caravan sewing garments. Swallow Tail, in spite of her father's treatment of her, was dutiful in taking care of him, even to the point of bathing his loins with asses' milk when he caught ailments from the village women. He would cry out in fever. Fish hooks and sharpened bamboo seemed to have invaded his loins. She was pained by his suffering, though she knew he deserved it.

Baoyu and Swallow Tail were inseparable, by instinct aware of each other's pulse, which was why they were a perfect pair for the knife-throwing act. Performers would come and go, becoming weak friends for a while, then strangers forever. Only Baoyu and Swallow Tail were constant. Of course, her higher social and physical standing prevented them from being bonded by stronger emotions. And Swallow Tail, having witnessed her father's deeds, had pledged from an early age never to be wedded. This resolution was reinforced whenever she went to the fields to pick mushrooms and came across circus performers in furtive love-making behind the trunk of a banyan tree.

"Give me your hand one last time," she said, dabbing coconut oil onto a cloth, stretching and wiping his fingers, one at a time, then massaging ash into them to make his hand dry. It was a ritual she'd enacted for many years before each knife-throwing performance to keep his fingers supple. This time she put aside the bowl of ash, unbuttoned her blouse and pressed his hand to her chest, until the oil left an imprint.

"Even when it fades it will never fade," she said, removing his hand and placing a purse into it, money stolen from her father. "Go now, go far from here, join another circus and when you throw knives at her think that it is me so that you will aim straight and not stray into more danger."

★

Danger. There was none, Baoyu's weakened eyesight brought an end to his knife-throwing career. He drifted from job to job, from master to master. He kept horses for this one, weeded the fields for that one. There were no more thrills , the knife flying through the air, cutting the cord that bound Swallow Tail, then quivering as it found wood. Gasps, then applause from the audience. He would walk calmly to the board to which Swallow Tail had been fastened, to retrieve his knives, but his veins were strained to bursting point and he could hear Swallow Tail's excited breath, and smell the sweat seething beneath the thick crust of her face powder. Night after night he and Swallow Tail had been coupled and uncoupled – the anticipation, the fear, the prospect of blood, the relief never waning, never settling into complacency.

Now, his knives were put to more sedate uses, cutting grass, or prising stones out of hooves. There was a stint at another circus, but this involved humiliation and not danger and a time of hazard before he was bought by Wang Changling. Since then, though danger had seemed to threaten when Sweet Li Jie and Ma Hongniang had arrived in the village with their tale of foreign invasion, this had not happened. Wang Changling had taken them in so readily, having longed for female companionship since the death of his mother, that Baoyu had feared he would be displaced in the household. Wang Changling had even seemed prepared to sacrifice his books to house the women.

"Make room for them in my study," he'd ordered Baoyu. Told him to move his chair, his desk, his shelf of books to the outhouse, not caring whether rain or sun rotted them, for it had only a broken roof. "Give them my bed; I will sleep on straw. Make a fresh stew for them. Give them towels, give them fans. Prepare my horse; I will ride to town to buy them fresh clothes." Baoyu was taken aback by his master's instructions. It was as if a falcon had fallen from the sky and lay fluttering outside their door. Wang Changling had so humbled himself in the presence of Sweet Li Jie and Ma Hongniang that Baoyu was left wondering what had wounded his master's mind. He had witnessed Wang Changling hunched over his writing, grieving, then tossing the pages aside, ordering a fire for them. He had been victim of Wang Changling's drunken songs; been surprised by his eccentric acts of kindness – to ants, to the serfs – but nothing had matched his concern for the two women. But if Baoyu's fear of abandonment was not realised, the presence of Sweet Li Jie and Ma Hongniang changed him for ever.

It happened when Ma Hongniang remembered her husband

and wept. Sweet Li Jie clung to her, and the sight of them was so piteous that Baoyu felt himself on the verge of emotion unbecoming to a knife-thrower, even a former one. Nerves contained, lips resolute, hand still... Baoyu suddenly realized that he had never cried in his life, except when, in his drunkenness, his mother had appeared in a dream to tell her dismal story. He vaguely remembered his father cuffing him for some misdeed, and village boys pelting him with stones, but such violence did not provoke tears. His childhood was normal in terms of bruises, rotting teeth, fevers, whippings from his father, but none of these had led to loss of face. Now, as he looked at Sweet Li Jie, he saw a child with knotted hair, broken nails and a face smeared with dirt. But he saw, too, a child lit up by sunlight, the dust escaping her skin like specks of white jade. He saw a child with a mother, and a missing father. He saw himself with a mother before the circus came for him. He could recall very little of his mother except that her hands always bore fruit and sweetmeats. He was always eating from her hands. The mother who appeared in his dream talked about scavenging the earth for worms and feasting on coal. She lied, for his memory was of fruit and sweetmeats. Why did she lie? Why did she sell him to the circus? Where was his father? Questions which he had sought to suppress for most of his life now arose because of the sight of Sweet Li Jie. He had no past and had doubted the scraps of memory that came to him, mostly when he was alone with Swallow Tail.

"You are all I have," he would blurt out, for a memory had suddenly visited him. He would go for months with a blank mind, occupying his time feeding and cleaning the circus animals or practising tricks with his knives to make the show more daring. Months and years, with only Swallow Tail for companionship, because the circus performers were jealous of his success and shunned him. So, when memory came, almost always about his mother, there was only Swallow Tail to share it with. "You are all I have," he said to her, denying the image of his mother which appeared in his mind.

Swallow Tail had taken his hand, leaned towards him and whispered, "What is it this time? Last month you were gorging on oranges you remembered your mother fed you. Here, close your eyes, open your mouth." She retrieved a plum from her pocket and placed it on his tongue. "Now chew. Is it as sweet as your mother's gift? Am I as sweet to you as your mother?"

Baoyu had lowered his eyes in shame. He wished he could express his feelings for Swallow Tail in words. Throwing his knife at her to free her from bondage was too violent and public an act. He wanted to whisper something to her more tender, more revealing of strong emotion. As it was, she pitied him, pitied his stunted frame, pitied his separation from family.

"I remember fruit trees everywhere," he said, chewing weakly on the plum Swallow Tail gave him, hiding the seed guiltily under his tongue.

"Fruits, fruits, eating from your mother's hand, that's all you talk about. There must have been more," Swallow Tail said. "Boys are bad. Short though you are, you must still have done wickedness. You must have raided your neighbours' stocks of corn. You must have had bloodied fights with other boys, with you throwing the stones and not them. You must have climbed a tree to feel like a man, even though bees made their hives in it. You must have stolen honey from beehives. You must have dug up earthworms and cut them in pieces to see how they still wriggled. You must have wrung the neck of a rabbit. You must have kicked over ants' nests to see them swarm out in shock. You must have caught a dragonfly and pulled out its wings. What else, let me think…"

★

Baoyu had been squatting in the doorway waiting for Wang Changling to return with new clothing for Sweet Li Jie and her mother. Sweet Li Jie reminded him of Swallow Tail, her round face, her bright black eyes, her dimpled chin, and the way her hair fell sideways over her shoulder like a splash of black paint. What had become of Swallow Tail? Was there a new knife-thrower to partner her? Baoyu grew jealous at the thought. He feared for Swallow Tail's safety in case the knife-thrower was a drunk or not sufficiently skilled. He strove to recall his last moments with her when she tended to the wounds inflicted by her father. What were his last words to her? He couldn't remember. In any case he was useless with words, not like Wang Changling. Perhaps his master would teach him to write, then he could send Swallow Tail a tender letter telling her about all his travels and his deeds since he left the circus. Of course, he would conceal the truth from her. He would not tell her that, asleep in the woods, he woke up to the cries of a traveller hauled from his horse by bandits, beaten about the head, robbed and left to die. When the bandits scooted off like satisfied wolves, Baoyu went up to the man but it was too late.

"Ma," the man had said in his delirium. "Ma, Ma," clutching Baoyu's hand with his final strength. Baoyu wiped his face with a wet cloth, rubbed water on his lips, raised his head for him to sip, and waited for him to die. Baoyu had no shovel to bury him. He dug his knife in the earth to make a hole, blunting the blade in the process. He covered him with branches and stones and went his way, wondering who the man's mother was and whether she would ever know his fate or be left pining for his return, stirring at the slightest noise and rushing to the door to greet him, only to be met with cold air, darkness, an owl hooting in pursuit of a rat.

Baoyu chose to remember the ills he had endured since he had left Swallow Tail; the new masters who worked him to exhaustion but refused to pay him as promised; the gangs who recruited him to pickpocket but bullied him out of his share of the booty. Worst of all was his engagement as a freak in a travelling show of other freaks. There were many booths. One contained a man with such abnormal nostrils that when he inhaled he threatened to suck in the scarves from around women's necks or lift their petticoats; another contained a boy with no arms and legs who was still able to bounce up and down as if handled by a puppeteer's strings; another, a creature, mostly male and partially female since he/she had two male organs and female genitalia: he/she was the star attraction and the show's best money-earner since both men and women crowded his/her booth, envious of his/her endowments, rubbing up against him/her to see how substantial they were and whether all three could be aroused in one go – and when they were, breaking out in delirious applause. The fourth booth displayed a tall woman. She had the small soft feet of a squirrel, but buttocks so huge that she easily lost her balance and toppled backwards; so huge that her hand could not reach them to wipe away perspiration that formed or insects which made their habitation in the foliage there. Her legs were permanently caked in her droppings. The booth stank. Her owner sold masks to spectators to supplement the small coins he charged for the viewing. Baoyu's space was the smallest, given his size. His role was to lie naked on his belly, a cloth covering his lower body. Children would approach and run their hands quickly along his back, terrified by the brevity of it and the bones pressing visibly against his skin. They would make him remove the covering and turn over so they could gawp at his testicles, tinier than cherry seeds and a bud of a penis which could not be aroused however long or ingeniously the children tickled it with bamboo sprigs specially provided by the owner.

In the hours between shows, Baoyu sought out the company of Buttocks, the woman's calling name.

"I will call you Swallow Tail, if you let me. It is the sound of a swallow rising in a rush of joy," Baoyu told her. He squatted beside her, his head almost at the same level as her buttocks. She lay on her stomach, unable to sit, for she would roll sideways. "May I call you Swallow Tail, or do you have another name? What did your parents call you when you were born?" Baoyu asked.

She said nothing but gazed at him as if she wanted to converse without words, as if words belonged to the world of flesh which was the source of her disgrace and banishment to a life in circuses. So Baoyu thought, wanting to be generous to her, as Swallow Tail had been generous to him. He could have deemed her dumb for that was how the owner introduced her to the spectators: "Born dumb, but her boulders speak volumes for her. Come forth, come peek, but not too close in case she cascades."

In the three months he spent in the show, every day found him in her company. To begin with he would tell her about his previous jobs, but his experiences were so dismal that he soon relented so as not to distress her more than she already was. Baoyu stopped talking to her. Even if he could invent happy stories to tell her, he would not, for they would only deepen her torment, evoking a way of being that she could never experience.

Instead of speaking to her, Baoyu started to take her hands into his, playing with her fingers to reassure her of his friendship. This proved uncomfortable for her – sprawled out on her belly, she needed to rest her palms on the ground to steady herself. Instead, Baoyu ran his fingers along the trough of her back. He took a cloth and wiped away the sweat gathered there. She seemed to cluck or gurgle as he did so, but this may have been his imagination. He continued to wipe her tenderly, more so when he remembered the women peeking at him over their fans, hiding their faces so as not to reveal emotion, stifling their merriment at his crotch, a fraction of the size of their husbands'. The women came to laugh, except one who stared at him gloomily. She was obviously used to copiousness because she brought her fifteen children with her. She stared at him in self-pity, thinking of her husband, a hulk of a man, looming over her in bed, then the inevitable births, the painful labour, the cycle repeated until she grew exhausted and in need of a walking stick. She visited regularly, and on the last occasion, she came without her children and her stick. She paid the owner for sole occupancy of the booth, and she squatted beside Baoyu for a full hour, not gazing at his crotch but into his eyes. He, too, saw her for the first time, noticing how her hair was combed and cunningly pinned back to hide a bald patch; how her neck was speckled with moles that gave it a beauty that made his tongue want to linger over them, like a child savouring sweets; how an old scar on her upper arm suggested she had once been stung by a centipede. When she left, she pressed a cloth of coins into his hand, taking out two pins from her hair to secure the opening, even though it exposed her baldness. Baoyu was grieved to see her go, the only woman except Swallow Tail who never laughed at him but found odd relief in the minuscule size of his crotch, after a lifetime of her husband's fluids bloating her body. She had seen beyond his lack and his deformity, or saw virtue in them. Baoyu began to strut about his booth with new vigour, stretching his back to straighten his posture and gritting his teeth at the pain. He determined to leave the freak-show before the term of his contract with the owner. He would compensate the owner with the woman's purse.

There was such an outgrowth of hair in the crevice of the tall woman's buttocks that Baoyu suddenly thought of the usefulness of the hairpins. Should he unfasten them from the purse and present them to Buttocks? Her hands, though, could not reach down that far, so Baoyu himself would have to neaten the outgrowth with the hairpins. Should he seek her consent before embarking on this exercise? How should he word it? And given that she would not answer, how would he proceed? Best to leave things alone, in their natural state, rather than risk offending her? He paused for a while, then made his decision. He moved down her body, and with the cloth soaked in her own sweat, to which he added his spittle, he began to cleanse her. What muck he could not budge with the cloth he dug up with his fingernails, brushed the flakes away. After a while of wiping and polishing, her buttocks shone. He was overcome with satisfaction. He removed the partition at the mouth of the booth to let sunlight scatter on them. If only she could witness her body! If only there was a mirror in the booth to persuade her of her beauty! He pressed on, loosening the clumps in her anal hair, combing his fingers through them, forming strands which could more easily be wiped clean. Pleased with his handiwork, he began making neat partings with the hairpins, a challenging task since he had never before been so intimate with a woman. Swallow Tail would sometimes rest her head in his lap as they sat under a tree eating figs and preparing for the night's performance. He was always too terrified to fondle her hair. He would look away to some distant point to dampen temptation.

★

Time for another parting. He knelt before Buttocks, muttered his farewell. She was wordless as usual, her breathing inaudible in spite of her weight. Only her eyes seemed to address him, but however deeply he peered into them he could not tell her true feelings. Her buttocks seemed to quiver when he rose to his feet to leave, but he put that down to his imagination. There were sores at the part of her belly which pressed most heavily on the ground – these were real enough, perhaps he should stay and tend to them. Swallow Tail would have wanted him to stay awhile. But the thought of more women coming to giggle at him behind their fans made him coarsen his heart. He gave the owner the purse of coins, beseeched him to apply plasters to Buttock's sores. The owner, snatching the purse, readily agreed. Baoyu left, knowing that nothing would be done.

The path away from the village where the circus was dwindled into three trails. Baoyu paused at the junction, deciding which one to take. He intuited that straight ahead was best, the way to an ordinary future. If he took the left trail his journeying would be beset by unspeakable ills. If he travelled on the right, his future would be uncertain, bringing him health or leprosy, longevity or swift execution. Swallow Tail would have wanted him to go straight, to live a simple but safe life, owning a plot of land, perhaps, growing enough to feed himself and needy neighbours, learning a skill like basket-weaving to bring him a regular income. Baoyu thought of Buttocks prostrate on the ground. The only reason for her existence was to whet men's appetite for deviancy. Was he himself not party to such foulness? He had polished her buttocks until they shone like the domes of a temple, and whilst there was no mischief in his mind, could he deny that he was aroused when he dug his hand into her crevice, the dirt raked up being from his own mind? Filth he was, and a freak. The owner was right to expose him to the gaze of normal folk.

He had chosen the left trail to punish himself. He met with grief and disgust, witnessed brawls, beheadings, folk chewing on bones, abandoned waifs, months when no moon appeared, no sun, the air choked with ash from scorched villages. He had grown callous from such experiences and had purged Swallow Tail and Buttocks, from his memory. The kindness and the pity Swallow Tail expected of him was senseless in such a world of slaughter. He'd become an animal alert to every threat, not venturing very far from its burrow, snatching at prey and hurrying back to safety where it could be devoured.

The left trail had ended at the marketplace where Wang Changling bought him and made a man servant of him in his fiefdom. He had become wary of a world which hurt him.

He remembered how Wang Changling drove briskly away from the market while he dangled his feet from the wagon, careless as to where he was being taken, careless of the sky bunched in black clouds, careless of the rain when it came.

"Cover my books," Wang Changling had urged, and for the first time Baoyu noticed what the wagon was carrying, apart from him: books! He had travelled with circus animals, sharing their cages before being rewarded with a wagon of his own for his lucrative skill at knife-throwing. Books! Never had he held one, much less kept company with so many! As the rain began to fall, he spread a cloth over them, the same cloth with which he had cleansed Buttocks, the same cloth which had covered his genitalia at the freak show, the same cloth which had wiped the face of the traveller slain by bandits. It had been Swallow Tail's gift, once patterned after a moth's wing, the dots of blue and grey threads long faded. She had spread it over him as he lay stricken by her father's blows. How often had he determined to patch the holes in the fabric, but his eyes were too poor to thread a needle and he was jealous of other hands and would not allow anyone to help repair her gift. Baoyu covered over the books, and, for more protection, he leant over the parcel, his curved back like a parasol against the rain.

As soon as they reached home, Wang Changling had put Baoyu to make soup while he sat on the floor, spreading his books around him, fumbling at them as at forbidden flesh, before deciding which he would read first. Baoyu stirred the pot of salted pork and onions, glancing at his new master furtively, curious as to what the book contained, noting the way the book was slanted to catch the best light, how the palm of the left hand curved to cushion it, how a finger was softened with saliva before it turned a page, how a different finger traced lines across the page, how legs twitched and toes curled, how legs were drawn up or spread out, how a breath was taken in deeply, then held for such a long time before escaping, how eyes were rubbed for clarity, chin stroked for concentration, mouth working up as if to utter, and then, with a huge yawn broken by a chortle of delight, the book was put down and Wang Changling clapped his hands.

★

Many nights passed before Baoyu felt safe in the company of his new master and then, his master in steady snore, he had crept to the cupboard and taken up a book. Such a dark incomprehensible deed! He had put back the book immediately in case it called out to wake Wang Changling. He waited an hour, goading himself to boldness before reaching for the same book, pressing it tightly between his palms to stifle any scream. No sound came. He opened it. Some spirit rushed to his head, swelled, burst, drenching him in sweat. He closed the book to dispel the spirit, replaced it in the cupboard, locked the cupboard, pulled the doors to make sure there were locked.

He went outside to recover, bracing himself against the wall, letting the winter breeze cut his face, freeze his sweat. The sky was subdued, barely a star, the moon like a seed sucked clean. A spirit of sadness entered him. At first he thought it was because he could never be like his master, skilled not just at reading but with all the gestures – hands, toes, legs, eyes, fingers and mouth orchestrated differently or in unison – that being with a book seemed to call for. For sure, such intimacy would be beyond him, as Swallow Tail was beyond him. He gritted his teeth to stem despair. Her voice came to him again. "You must have pelted stones at a wasp nest, torn off the wings of a dragonfly, wrung the necks of rabbits…" She had rested her head in his lap, closed her eyes. He looked out at an early moon slicing through clouds in frantic pursuit of… nothing. What was there to chase? Thoughts bigger than himself boomed in his mind; he could not find words to express them, even badly. Swallow Tail's hair was as lush as a sky of early stars. That was all he could say – if he'd had the courage to speak. The rest of his thoughts were wisps of questions forming and dissolving that had to do with his future. He could not understand them and they caused him sudden anxiety. He went to stand up, to ease memory of Swallow Tail away from him, to stop the questions that trailed accusations and doubt in their wake. She was stubborn, though. She resisted, pressing her head more firmly in his lap, not even bothering to open her eyes.

"The night sky is so… so…" Swallow Tail had said, trying to find a fresh description. "You know what I mean," she sighed. "You are the only person who knows what I mean, always."

Baoyu's face creased. He was glad she had not been able to see his eyes reddening.

"Well, what have you to say?" she asked. He took a long time to stifle his feelings. He had to summon up a jumble of images to clear his mind and make it incurious as to why the moon was in haste, why the stars were early, why moon and stars were there at all. But really the question had been why Swallow Tail was laid out before him like light itself, why there was flesh to her beauty that could not be gathered up, pressed to his lips.

"Well what have you to say? You are the only person who knows what I mean."

"Mean? Mean?" he stuttered. "What do you mean by 'mean'?"

She'd opened her eyes and beamed at him. "Oh my bright boy! So bright! You understand everything but you pretend to be dull."

Braced against the wall, Baoyu let the rough stone bruise his back to distract himself from memory of Swallow Tail's praise. He tried to summon up a jumble of images, unrelated, contradictory, to displace her – the broken axle of a wagon, though the inside was lined with fine furs; a table with a missing leg, though it bore a dainty tea set; a juggler's hands infected with sudden pus who yet could throw and catch without spillage. Such things he had witnessed in the circus and in his voyaging through villages, but they had never before left an imprint in his mind. Now, inexplicably, they surfaced to protect him from dwelling on Swallow Tail. She resisted again, as he knew she would, refusing to leave his mind. Nothing would budge such a wilful creature from his mind! This time it was her voice that probed him about Buttocks.

"Bright! How you polished her! But you thought she was mute. How could you be so arrogant?"

He went to protest but she hushed him.

"She was saying many things to you. She was asking after the why of the moon and the stars, and the why of her buttocks. And did you ever not think that she might have been secretly proud of herself, that at least there was something which marked her out, drew crowds to her? You sensed only pain in her, which was always there, but why not pride too? Why did you not see her as normal in her abnormality? Why did you see her, like the crowds, as a freak?"

This was right about Buttocks, he thought, pressing himself against the frosty stone wall, this time to distract himself from her imagined charges.

Baoyu went back inside. Wang Changling was still in a deep snore. What to do? He was too disturbed to sleep. Should he desert Wang Changling, saddle up the swiftest horse to seek out

Buttocks, but to do what with her? Wang Changling would send men to retrieve him. When he was back in the village, Wang Changling would starve him, then force pepper into his mouth. Even feed him with pig faeces. Baoyu listened to his master's snore, wondering whether he was capable of enduring such punishment. Wang Changling had already promised to make him scream and faint when his arms were branded with a hot iron. Baoyu accepted such treatment as a creature owned and needing to be marked. Wang Changling was acting properly. Feeding him faeces would also be just chastisement for absconding with the best horse.

What to do about Buttocks? The book cupboard mocked him. If only he could compose a letter to Swallow Tail, seeking her advice and comfort! A letter in which he disclosed to her the many hours he had spent puzzling over the why of Buttocks and the why of stars. He was not as broken-minded as everybody deemed him to be, just because of his body. He was not as wise as his master but he could still grapple with curious thoughts. If grapple was too boastful a term, then spar or scratch would do. Whatever the correct word, Swallow Tail would know. She knew most things about him and what she didn't, she would guess at. He resolved to write her not one but three letters. The first would be simple, wanting guidance about Buttocks. The second would be more complicated, telling her of his adventures since leaving her but withholding most of the nastiness. The third would be the longest. He would recall all his thoughts about why he was alive, why others were alive, why all would turn to smut, char, foul air, but mostly it would be about his feelings for her, feelings which, somehow, would survive. It would take years to master the craft of writing, but when he did so he would be as fluent as in his knife-throwing. He knew Swallow Tail loved him; she would wait for his letters forever if needs be.

CHAPTER TWO
Swallow Tail's Dream

"Boys are bad," she had said to Baoyu. "You must have done wickedness. You must have raided your neighbours' stocks of corn. You must have had bloodied fights with other boys, with you throwing the stones and not them. You must have climbed a tree to feel like a man, even though bees made their hives in it. You must have wrung the neck of a rabbit. You must have kicked over ants' nests to see them swarm out in shock. You must have caught a dragonfly and pulled out its wings. What else, let me think..."

She paused to contemplate all the adventures she wished she had embarked upon as a girl. Running away and hiding in a clump of bush, with a basket of carrots and dried fish to last a week. Ignoring the desperation of her father as he walked through the woods calling out her name; the search party at night, with their torches to guide them, but also to ward off attacks by snakes and wolves. Her father was a coward, he sent others at night to find her, remaining secure in his bed with somebody's wife. She thought of running away to the woods where she could swim in the river, fish darting between her thighs, and afterwards lying on the bank to dry off and fall asleep in a wrap of sunlight. She would cast off her clothes and walk naked through the woods and the creatures would be stilled by the paleness of her skin, the cherry scent of her flesh, the raw perfume of her hair. The otter would place a fish in her path, the bear would bring honey, the monkey would lead her to a nest of eggs. But if they kept to their natural ways, no matter. Let the snake strike, let her fall to the ground and lie there for days, consumed by fever, her limbs swollen, her mouth dry. Let the wolf pounce, stopping her heart or making it beat so frantically that it burst out of her chest to be lapped up or fought over by other animals. And if she did not escape to the woods, then it would be to a faraway village. She would descend from a hill, bleeding. Someone would rush up to her, lift her on his back, take her to his home. His wife would wash her, bandage her wounds, feed her, let her sleep for days on end. When she was restored to health she would repay their kindness, sewing and knitting for them, and letting the man fondle her when his wife was asleep. Or pretending to be asleep, glad that her husband was being pleasured in ways her toilworn body did not wish to perform. The wife would be so grateful to Swallow Tail that she made sure that Swallow Tail was fed first, a plate of fried bananas each morning, and if she so wished, did not have to work. She could idle all day in the house, admiring her reflection in a brass pot, painting and repainting her nails, sucking an orange and spitting out the seeds to see how far they could reach. Boredom would set in and her blood would call for new adventures.

"You have been a thousand strands of silk to me," Swallow Tail would say, praising her hosts and expressing her intent to leave. The wife would be taken aback. Her bottom lip would tremble and she'd burst out crying. "Stay at least another night. Give us time to prepare a bag of belongings for you to safeguard your journey." Swallow Tail would agree and hug her to banish her tears.

Swallow Tail would go to bed as usual, succumbing to the man's massage, even sighing and squirming to feign pleasure and restore his sense of vanity. She would fall into a deep sleep because the wife had laced her tea with special powders. When she woke she'd go to stretch out her arms, but find them bound by ropes to the bed post. "You are our slave now," the wife would say with a glee and venom completely at odds with her previous character. She took up a stick and beat Swallow Tail furiously, stopping only because of exhaustion. The man looked on, but with shame in his eyes. Now and again he made a cautious attempt to intercede, but his wife brushed him aside. "Tie her to the roof-beam," the wife commanded, thrusting rope into his hand. "She can move about the room, do my cooking and cleaning and washing, but gag her mouth so she cannot alert the neighbours."

Swallow Tail dreamt how the wife spent the night plotting her own escape from household servitude and how she, Swallow Tail, would replace her. The wife could then set up a stall in the market place to sell vegetables. Oh how easy a task, bathed by the sun and engaging in banter with her customers! She could expand her stall, to offer household goods, cups, plates and the like. Free from domestic chores, she could work more hours, undercut her competitors, make more profit. Money would accumulate, and another stall and then a third could be set up. Eventually, she could retire, renting her stalls out to receive a steady income. With the money she would buy fine dresses to strut around the village, as the richer women did, waving their hands to show off her bride-bangles. They were born into plenty, they owned herds of goats, ducks, geese.

No, there was more to this story. The wife would decide that the money should be spent on her parents, banished to a leper's hovel outside the boundary of the village. For all their lives her parents had ploughed their rice fields with hired oxen, making just enough to sell some grains and stave off malnutrition. With scraps for clothes, they had eaten with their hands from water-lily leaves, because plates were beyond their income. They fed their only child – the wife-to-be – first, begged the teacher to give her a space in the village school, if only until she could learn to count to fifty. No need to go beyond fifty; there would never be more than fifty bundles of rice to sell or exchange for vegetables, and there would never be more than fifty – much less, but they could dream – onions or tomatoes to grace their pots in a week's cooking. They placed all their future in their daughter, marrying her when she was fourteen to a carpenter. He only had four fingers, the rest lost to the chisel over the years. The number four was ominous to many, so no one else would marry him, though he had inherited his parents' small house, but with a bed, a table, a chair, a wardrobe, a wash basin… Twenty legs of furniture all together, more than usually expected of a suitor. Then there were the goats, fifteen in all, another sixty legs. Eighty altogether, ten times the lucky number eight.

The marriage was happy, though no children came. Husband doted on wife, making goat-milk cheese to delight her mouth, and when a kid was born, they would name it after the child they could not bear. Soon they had many bleating offspring and they felt blessed. They painted and repainted the shrine in their yard to give thanks to the gods. But the gods were brutes because leprosy struck the village. Many died but the daughter kept her parents alive by herbal medicine bought from the neighbouring town and eggs mixed with castor oil. A goat was sold for a month's supply, then another, then another. Soon they were all gone, including the kids. The leprous parents were saved from death but sent away beyond the edge of the village.

The daughter had heard there was a new cure for leprosy and was on the brink of selling the furniture to pay for it when Swallow Tail arrived. The gods had relented. The gods had heeded her prayers, her offerings of duck eggs to the effigies in the shrine. Swallow Tail would be her means to new wealth and the restoration of her parents to village society. She would have to beat her regularly to break her will, but she would also make sure Swallow Tail was well fed.

When her parents were finally cured and Swallow Tail sufficiently fattened, the wife would offer her utmost gift to the gods. On a moonless night, when the villagers were asleep, husband and wife would bind her hands, her feet, bash her head in with a stone. They would roll her body in a white cloth, lift her to the shrine and gouge her throat with the very chisel that had ruined her husband's hand, making him unable to build more than one table and chair a month. Swallow Tail's blood would be sprinkled over the gods, and she would be buried whilst there was still breath in her as a living and eternal slave to the earth. The husband's fingers would grow back, his subtle hands crafting so much furniture that wealth was assured. Goats would be bought to graze the land, because Swallow Tail's body was renewing and fertilizing the soil.

★

To give succour to the earth! Swallow Tail beamed at the thought, feeling proud of her destiny. She lay on her imagined bed, trussed up so tightly she could barely move. If only Baoyu could suddenly appear, batter down the door, toss his knife at the rope, slice her free. If only it was Baoyu's hand roving over her body rather than the husband's. Although she gasped when the husband pinched

75

her nipples and afterwards softened the pain with his tongue, although she pretended to relish his love making, Swallow Tail was numb within. It was only when she thought of Baoyu that the husband's clumsy and apologetic hands came to life and she imagined how she strained against the rope, twisting here and there until a surge of energy almost lifted her out of the bed, body taut, face contorted, mouth opened, before she slackened, fell back into repose, sweat softening the rope against her skin. The husband stopped fondling her, taking sudden fright at her transformation. Thinking he had brought her to the brink of death, he quickly loosened the knots, untangled her, took up a fan to cool her face, fetched water for her burning lips.

"My wife, " he muttered. "My wife... Her mother and father, they have leprosy... She's grown crazy with grief... I am sorry. Here, let me free you. We will not sacrifice you to the gods." He took away her soiled clothing and came back with a new dress and a purse of coins. "My wife... she sleeps... Go now before she awakens... Go!" He held up his hands to Swallow Tail to show his missing fingers and gain her pity...

...Go? Go where? To whom? Back to her father's wagon? To Baoyu? But Baoyu had long gone, wandering the earth in search of a miracle to restore his battered eye so he could throw straight again. She would set off to find him, and when she did she would surely lie beside him, rest his head in her lap, tease his spine until it grew straight. If she massaged his legs they would lengthen. Light would be restored to his eye and his jawbone would be healed. She would behold him in his changed state and marvel at her gifts. But after a while she would grow accustomed to his normal appearance and succumb to boredom. She would long for his ugliness again. It was his deformed frame which had excited curiosity and dared her to intimacy, dared her to disobey her father. No, she would not venture after him. Let him stay blighted and in need of a miracle, moving through the land, devouring herbs from this healer and that, and when all failed and he was penniless, let him lie down on the bare earth and look up to the sky, wanting the clouds to blacken and burst and floods sweep him away to a ravine into which he would fall, crack his head against rock and find sleep forever. If the clouds refused to destroy him, remaining pitiless and white, then let new vigour make him arise from the bare earth, let him set off again in search of strange stones under which lived…? What fantastic creatures would he uncover under these stones? A serpent uncoiling, darting at him, fangs piercing his feet, poison racking his body until it grew straight? An invisible insect entering a crevice in his foot sole, stealing into his body, laying eggs which hatched and blossomed and gave flesh to his spine and an abscess to round off his jaw? No, she would not go to Baoyu but leave him to stumble upon magical stones in caves, mountains and deserts; and if there were none to be found, let him climb trees and taunt the wasps or sharp-toothed lizards that lived there so they could assault him, each bite and sting strengthening his body. It was pain he sought, inflicted not by animals but by love. His father had cuffed him, boys had pelted stones at him, the circus master had broken his jaw, but he was numb to such violence. Only she had aroused him to pain when he was forced to leave her. He had put on a blank face but felt his bones being broken, one by one, by some devil within. He had limped away, aroused by the pain of loss. Unbearable loss, bearable pain. How more noble and defiant to die than breed the stoicism to make such pain bearable!

★

"Go now, take this purse before she wakes up," the husband whispered, pushing Swallow Tail towards the door with his four active fingers. She resisted him and looked back longingly at the rope and the unclean bed. She needed to be humiliated anew, so she left the village and set out for the colony of lepers, curious as to how they managed from one day to the next, knowing that their flesh was uncertain and wondering what part of the body would peel away that afternoon or the next day. In the leper village she would scour the woods for herbs to ease their discomfort. She would strip tree bark to make bandages for them. But she found them dour. They stared out morosely from the doorways of their makeshift homes, hardly speaking to each other for fear (she surmised) that their jaws might slacken with too much motion. There were no stories to be had from them and after a week their sores were no longer spectacular. Before she left, she took up a shovel and dug many graves for them, the aches from moving so much earth her only means of connecting to their affliction.

Her mind roved to another place. She tore her dress, rubbed ash on her face and took up a position outside the market to beg. The sun beat down on her bare head, her arms stiffened agonisingly from being stretched out for hours. Rain came to soak her but she stayed put, watching the way her body shivered as if it was not her own. She was steady within, determined in her new calling. Some threw scraps for her but she let the stray dogs devour them. A child came up to her to stare but then howled, the mother dragging her away. Men turned away their faces when they passed her, but the young women were kind, giving her coins as if to ward off a dismal future. She spoke pleasing words to them and asked the gods to keep them comely. A week in the same spot, not sleeping a wink... People began to marvel at her endurance. They deemed her to be special, a sorcerer disguised in rags. They showered her with gifts of fruit, for such unearthly beings shunned meat. They reached out to touch her though her skin was ruined by scabs. They beseeched her to tell their fortunes.

"You will marry a brave soldier who will serve you with all his strength," she told one. "He will survive many battles and bring home booty enough to last eight lifetimes." Such a prophecy gave glee to all, because Swallow Tail told them that the abundance of one would be shared with others.

But there was a malcontent, named Caihong. There was nervousness in her eyes. Her smile was false. She was the prettiest among the young women, upturned breasts, rich lips, radiant skin, hair a coverlet of silk. Caihong was wary of her good looks which made her vulnerable to malicious gossip from rivals, and an early marriage to an elderly man, Dong Dong, who could not satisfy her but who furnished her family with plenty, being the owner of a coal mine. For her, though, a bleak future because the husband was barely virile. Others tried to seduce her and she surrendered.

"The spring breeze blowing into my skirt was a man unknown to me," she said. She was thrilled by men's handling of her, but afterward the loneliness was unbearable. Days and nights hungering for the sweat, the delirium, and love bites, wondering who the next stranger would be. She was careful not to sleep with anyone local, going to markets in distant towns which sold goods of sufficient value and quality to maintain her prestige among the villagers, and which necessitated overnight visits. There, she would choose a stall holder, a man of lowly status but of good physique.

"Bring these goods wrapped nicely to my hotel," she would say, throwing her money at him and walking away, spurning the change in a show of superiority. That way he was duty-bound to serve her in bed. When he arrived at her hotel room, she opened the door dressed only in undergarments. He would be speechless and try to turn away, but she would seize his arm and with unexpected strength pull him into the room, where she would threaten to get him jailed for attempting to assault her, a stranger far from home, a vulnerable woman, his social better. He had no choice but to comply with her scheming, all night obeying her every whim and command, until she was satisfied and satisfied again. She would dismiss him with the warning that she would report him to the authorities should he ever utter a word about their doings.

"Tell your wife you got drunk and fell asleep in a field," she would say, gesturing to the door. "I will return when I am ready, I expect you to be here."

There was a baby but it died before birth. The elderly husband was pleased when Caihong's belly started swelling. He had lain on top of her on a few occasions and she had been gracious in accepting his withered excrescence, so he credited himself with her pregnancy. She cried and cried when the baby was stillborn, no amount of gifts – new dresses, ornaments, furniture – could console her. She blamed herself, for she had continued to sleep with men after being alerted to the pregnancy. The more her belly grew, the more she hungered for the company of strangers, one of whom might have released the germ which she thought had killed the baby. Caihong had only stopped crying when Swallow Tail appeared in their midst. She was nervous in Swallow Tail's presence but a craving for contact suffused her eyes. Swallow Tail knew she was desperate to leave the village and loveless marriage, and rumours were growing about her escapades during her shopping trips. One of her victims, enraptured by her beauty, her deliciousness in bed, must have boasted to his friends about the tryst.

"Come, let me whisper in your ear," Swallow Tail told Caihong. "There is a land far away in a new kingdom of the earth. The Land of Gold. The emperor and princes there wear garments draped with gold. Go there, go to such splendour, but you must cross many waters before you arrive. No woman from this province, much less this village, has ever journeyed there. You will become a legend. From now on, forget your name, take another. From now on you will be called Pioneer."

Pioneer was aghast. She had expected a lighter intervention from Swallow Tail, perhaps a yearlong sojourn with her husband in another province, only a week's journeying away.

"What is the name of the new land? How far away? How will I get there? How can a woman venture abroad alone? Who will guide me? Who will protect me?"

Swallow Tail continued to whisper in her ear. "Your husband will take you. I will send him dreams of women walking naked through the forest, for the women in New Land wear no clothes, such is the warmth of the sun and such the shameless culture. The trails through the forest are littered with gold nuggets. You will gather so much that you will need donkey and cart to carry them. When your husband awakens from his dreams he will be desperate to go to New Land. The wealth! The women! He will force you to go with him, but you must first protest so that your village will feel pity for you and think of you as a woman wronged. They will quickly forget the rumours about your adultery, they will side with you, urging your husband not to take you away to savage climes. Of course, your husband will keep quiet about the gold and the flesh of his dreams, in case the whole village, the whole province, the whole country follow him to share in the bounty. He will want it all for himself. Is that not why he is a rich man? Has he ever given away any of his goats, any of his stock of corn, or coal from his mine to his inferiors, at harvest time or the spring festival? The villagers will recall his miserliness, they will deem it even more disgraceful that he should seek to remove you from their company. They will recall every act of kindness you showed them, however small. Do you remember giving women cakes to feed the gods when the full moon came? Do you remember giving two books to the school mistress to help her teaching? Do you remember, when your baby died, how you refused to eat for days and days, telling your servant to take the food for her family? These meagre gifts will become magnified in their minds; they will deem you their veritable champion and will curse your husband for taking you away, depriving them of your charity, paltry as it was. Protest, but in the end give way to your husband. The villagers will wail as you leave, they will shower you with petals. In your absence, stories will arise about you, each one adding detail to the other. As time passes, you will become a legend. You will have your own shrine which will be festooned with flowers on the anniversary of your departure. You will have your own petitioners seeking your blessing on matters of health and money."

Pioneer listened, feeling despondent and excited by turns. When she thought of the hardships ahead – the strangeness of New Land, the primitive natives, even the lack of dumplings – she pulled away to catch her breath, but Swallow Tail drew her back.

"Are you not a strong woman? Have you not deceived your husband so often? New Land will hold many dangers but you are habituated to risks, no?"

Pioneer blushed. She sucked in her lips, signalling to Swallow Tail to stop speaking.

★

More weeks at the same spot, rain or shine, and not a wink of sleep for Swallow Tail as she squatted at the market. They came at all hours, not only the young but women of all ages, men too. She gave babies their names and the elderly who hobbled up on sticks went away with firm backs and new blood erasing the blue from their veins. The men stood and stared, too nervous to confess their sins, but the women beseeched her for her understanding or her forgiveness. One said: "I was one of the many who put sand in my girl-child's nostrils, and when she was suffocated I left her in the open field for vultures to peck. They flew off with pieces of her to the heavens, where the land is green, the air and water unsullied. The birds planted her there so she could revive and

81

grow into a maiden of such buxom sweetness that the gods will vie for her favours."

Another said, "My father minded hogs more than he minded us. He spent all day with them in the woods as they foraged for frogs. When he brought them home, he took hours to wash them, remove ticks and twigs, give fat friendly pats on their buttocks, wish them a happy sleep. Do hogs dream? My father believed they did. 'Did you dream last night of a ditch of dead rats, did you gorge until not a single tail or whisker was left?' he asked the hogs. He was particularly fond of one sow. He'd say to her 'Did you dream of me? Did you follow me all day through the woods, stopping when I stopped, running when I ran? When I fell asleep, did you stand guard over me, flicking away flies with your lusty tail?'

"After a while we women resented him for giving all his affection to the sow. One evening, my father had a stroke and toppled over in the pigsty. He was in sleep for three months. When he stirred, the first thing he asked for was his favourite sow. But we had already slaughtered it, fed on it for days, my mother sucking on its eyes, savouring the jelly – the eyes which once gazed coyly at her husband. We sold off the rest, bought new and rich clothing, oils for our skin, ornaments for our hair, mattresses to lie on. We knew that news of the hacking and dispersal of his hogs would kill him. It did. We cried and then we laughed. We roasted a hen and drank pomegranate juice. We missed him at first but then forgot him.

"But he returns to haunt us. In our dreams, he wears a sow's head. He stares at me. He does not speak. In another dream he comes as a butcher's knife, with the handle bearing the image of his face. He re-enacts how we slit his favourite sow's throat and held it over a bucket to bleed. Oh the horrible, horrible squealing, kicking against the rope – so long for it to die! But in truth the meat was tasty. How we feasted, and made spicy soups with the bones! Oh joy! Shame came afterwards, the burping done, the belly deflated. We looked at each other with guilt in our eyes, not daring to speak to each other. Even now, years later, only a few words pass between us. My sister did marry but to a simple farm-hand, and she moved away with her new family. Not far, but even though she needs money she rarely visits. My mother seemed to age rapidly. Her teeth slackened; one by one they fell out. She does not relish meat any more. I bury each tooth before our shrine but the gods have cursed us for our father's death. As for me, what can I tell you? We had wealth, cows and hens and a thriving garden, but men shunned me. Word had spread about our father's untimely death. I hate hogs, I hate them! In the daytime I see them rolling in the mud, not a care about the future, whereas I am always fearful for my mother's health, on the lookout for a husband. I wish I could throw stones at the pigs I see, stamp upon their babies until life is squashed out through their nostrils, but I dare not in case the god of pigs hastens our end."

Swallow Tail patted her cheeks to pacify her, stroked her face and in a gentle voice told the woman to convert to another view of pigs. "They care for their young, even if they are female. They eat our leftovers, they clear our gutters of all manner of vermin, which in their stomachs is transformed into new flesh, new bones, to satisfy our hunger. They turn muck into the means to keep us alive and healthy. Go forth with new vision, purchase a piglet, nurture it, adopt it as your first child, feed it from your palm, it will bring you forgiveness and fortune. One day, a man will pass your house. He will see you cuddling the animal, fondling its chin, pressing its lips to yours, squeezing its sides until it squeals with laughter. That man will have had a hard, loveless life. Perhaps he was born in a ditch and left to die there until someone rescued him and traded him for a basket of plums. Or perhaps he grew up in richness but his body harboured a sickness which no one could understand, much less cure; a sickness that visited much pain on him regularly, which made him curse himself, damn the gods, breed cruelty in his heart. Then by sheer chance he sees you with your first child , the piglet, and he is so moved by your adoration of the animal that he will enter your house, propose to you on the spot. You will have restored him to grace, in spite of the pain of his illness. You will live happily with many offspring, though the first child, your piglet, will be the ornament of your family. No longer will silence reign in your house. Children giggling, chattering, rattling, tattling. Even your mother – she will be like their choir mistress and conductor of words."

The woman pressed Swallow Tail's hands into hers and wept with new cheer. She searched her pocket for a coin of gratitude but Swallow Tail refused and sent her away with even more sweet, false words.

Hardly a pause, when another woman rushed up to Swallow Tail to unburden herself. Her face was veiled. She spoke of her enduring love and loyalty to her husband. She was so fortunate to be with him, she blessed her parents for making such a godly match. "I loved my husband too much, but too much was not enough, so I strove to love him even more. Each morning I woke up early to make the best rice cakes and dumplings for him. When he returned from the fields – we were prosperous with cows – there were bowls of vegetable stews for him, freshly baked meat pies, the table furnished with tofu curds and lichen. A boy child came and then another. We were content. No, we were more than content, we rejoiced in each other's company, our lovemaking was as fresh and bewildering as on our marriage night... Until I changed. Why? How did it come about? Did some mischievous spirit enter my heart? Did my neighbours cast a spell on me out of envy? I don't know. I've questioned myself a thousand times a day but no reason comes to me. I still cared for my children, I still cooked my husband the best cakes, I still made love to him with the clumsiness that comes with overexcitement. Still, in the midst of gladness I doubted. He was so dashing, so young, so affluent... I began to imagine other women in his life. When he spent hours in the distant fields, minding the cows, did he sneak away to some woman's bed? When he returned home in happiness, was it in anticipation of the next day's meeting with his lover? When he made love to me with such zest, was he thinking of her?"

The woman said she would secretly examine his naked body for evidence of illicit sex when he slept. A scratch on his back or a bruise on his neck... Had she caused this during their own coupling or was it his lover's doing? Her lovemaking changed. She no longer seized him, she no longer gave herself up to arousal and climax. She became thoughtful in her movements. She touched him softly so as not to leave marks on his body. Each night, when he undressed, she asked him innocently about this bruise, that discoloration. He said he'd tripped over a stone, or grazed himself against thorn bushes. She disbelieved him but remained dutiful in bed. Only once did she betray her feelings, turning away from him so his mouth soured on her breast. He was confused. She turned back to him, out of guilt, and let him suckle on her. He sensed her reluctance, he failed to be aroused. "You're tired, you've laboured too much for us, cooking, cleaning, caring for our children. Tomorrow we will hire a wagon and holiday in a far valley. Go to sleep," he said, hugging her to his chest, fondling her hair, wiping away a tear that dripped from her.

She continued to doubt him but was as obliging as ever in bed and in the home. One day a sore appeared on her inner lip. It hurt for three days, then waned. Every other month thereafter, like an errant star, it appeared, again only briefly, before withdrawing. She took it as punishment for her jealousy. Her poor husband! He dedicated his life and goods to her, he deserved a wife more worthy than her. She chided herself for wronging him in her mind. She resolved to cleanse herself of distrust. The sore persisted. It spread along the whole of her inner lip. It leaked. She took to wearing a veil to conceal the pus.

"What can I do to rid me of jealousy?" she begged Swallow Tail. "My husband adores me still, he tolerates what would be odious to other men. The sore makes my breath stink, but he still seeks my lips at night. I am a wretch. He should withdraw from me to another wife."

Swallow Tail lifted the veil to examine the sore. She recognized immediately it was caused by sexual infection. How often had she tended to her father when he had been similarly afflicted? And many of the circus performers, because of loose behaviour in each village they visited, caught the same germ. Swallow Tail could have told the woman the truth about her husband's disloyalty. He had indeed absconded from the cow pasture to frolic with a local whore, engaging in acts so taboo that they could not be named. She could have reassured the woman that her husband was normal in his behaviour. He meant no harm to her and remained devoted. It was just that when the gods composed men, an invisible worm settled in the pure clay as it was drying, burrowing deep inside. It was the deed of a fiendish god who quarrelled with the others over rulership of the skies. He was expelled to the very edge of the universe, to a space so dark that invisibility was a natural state. He vowed to topple the rule of his fellow gods. His first act of malice was to infect the clay out of which a man was made. "Blame the fiend, blame the worm," Swallow Tail could have said, explaining that men were visited by desires too lusty and delinquent to be enacted upon a wife, never mind one who was a mother. Only with a stranger and with the payment of impersonal coin could a man stage and act out the imaginations of his lust. It would take ten seasons to bring his performance to an end, and for the worm to expire. No, a wife and a mother could never be involved in such a vile drama.

Swallow Tail could have said all of this and the woman might have understood. But Swallow Tail decided to tell her a comforting lie to reconcile her to her husband. She would send her away, too, with an actual remedy for her sore. As she was formulating her lie – it took time for it had to be convincing and final – a beggar woman appeared from nowhere and emptied a gourd of warm urine over Swallow Tail's head.

"We all added our bit, we all took turns with the gourd until it was brimful," the beggar woman boasted to the crowd that had gathered around Swallow Tail, waiting their turn to confide in her.

Her fellow beggars pushed their way to the front and glared at Swallow Tail. "You have robbed us of our livelihood," one accused. "No one gives us alms anymore, they give all to you." "This is my spot," another said, pushing Swallow Tail away with her one hand. "I've been begging here since a suitor chopped me, twenty years ago. Go back to your own village; you are not one of us." The crowd queuing to meet Swallow Tail protested on her behalf. A man took up a stone and threatened the beggars. They stayed for a while sulking, then withdrew, casting evil looks at Swallow Tail.

Time to leave, Swallow Tail decided. She had given blessings, named children, listened to lies, love stories, heard about the sow that bode ill and defended its virtue; dreamt the carpenter who caressed her, the lepers, and much more. Enough adventures for the time being. Time to leave, to go back to her circus wagon, to go back to sewing, knitting, bathing the circus animals, cleaning their pens, back to routine and the hollow emotion of watching the jugglers, the acrobats performing their regular acts and their furtive lovemaking behind banyan trees. Back to her irate father, his whips, his victims. Back to a lonely bed, hoping for Baoyu's return. Back to being awake.

PART FOUR

CHAPTER ONE

Undated letters from Suitor Jia Yun

Dear Sweet Li Jie, many thousands of Chinese arrived in Demerara in the decades before me, but I don't mix with them. As soon as their period of bonded labour expired, they either lazed or went into business – charcoal and opium to begin with. They dug pits in the jungle, cut down the best hardwood trees and made charcoal in such a bulk that there were not enough boats to ferry it along the river to the city, Georgetown. Such was the demand and so sharp their dealings (late in paying boat owners; late in paying money lenders) that quite a few made small fortunes. Some invested in opium shipped from China, the dens doubling up as gambling houses. In them, all day, you can see Chinese throwing bamboo dice and hollering. Stabbings were rife in such places, the police every so often having to draw their guns to quell the mayhem.

After a few months in the Colony, word must have got out about my new but profitable business. A man named Chen visited me. He was dressed in the Chinese way, with pigtail, wide cotton trousers hiding a knife, long and tapering at its end, and leather-soled slippers with canvas straps, but his watch and finger rings told of his standing. A horse-drawn carriage waited on him.

"Not far, not far," he said when I asked from where he'd come. "I live two hours away, but the road!" He brushed his trousers to remove dust. "I come to bring you good proposal," he said, launching into a description of his business and the wealth he had accumulated. He smiled to show his teeth. He obviously scraped them with charcoal, then cleansed and polished them. I presumed his display of shiny teeth was to augur my future should

I join up with him. "You can make more money in charcoal than cloth," he said, pressing me for an investment. "My technique and secret recipe make the best charcoal in the Colony. I use coconut shells mixed in with particular trees that only I know about, which we harvest deep in the jungle. Other people go cheap; they use the nearest trees, too afraid to set up operation in the jungle."

"Cloth is my calling," I told him, but smiled and offered him a cup of milk and a plate of watermelon. Men like Chen had a reputation for ready violence (Harris had briefed me on this), so I was afraid he might yank my pigtail and draw his knife at my refusal.

"I see you have clean hands, countryman, but the charcoal won't dirty you up. We don't do the job, we take on hungry-belly buck people who barely have enough turtle meat and labba to eat. We pay these Carib savages with plenty-plenty liquor; they sign contract paper with their thumb print. Right away you have fifty slaves."

I smiled and nodded as if approving his business ways, but I despised his scorn for the native people who had yielded land to him and toiled for him, no doubt for miserly dollars. He made other attempts to part me from my money. I listened carefully to keep the peace. He munched on the last slice of melon, gazing at me as if I was a fool. When he left, the carrion crows were still circling and the parakeets and macaws were making such a noise you'd think it was a murder scene.

No one came with a proposition about opium; they must have heard that I neither smoked nor drank and that all my habits are as clean as my hands.

★

Dear Sweet Li Jie, I will tell you about the two Demerara men who have made my life bearable; who have helped me in my commerce; who have told me about the nature of the local fish, fowl, flowers; who have taught me about Coolie Hindu practices and Muslim ghazals – and a lot more.

Meeting Negro Harris
Harris knocked on my door early one morning as I was practising shining my teeth with a charcoal sample Chen had presented to

me. I rinsed my mouth quickly and went to see who it was. "An ocelot strayed into your yard, it died and it smelling up the place," he said. " I smelt it from afar."

It was my first encounter with him. I looked him up and down, noticing first the nature of his clothing – khaki cotton trousers full length; half-sleeved cotton shirt, blue, with a top button missing – then his feet which, though slippered, were padded with calluses, suggesting a man who had walked far.

"I was just passing. I thought I'd stop and tell you it's a rotting ocelot, not your latrine."

I was taken aback. When I saw he was looking curiously at my face, I wiped the side of my mouth and discovered some grains of charcoal on my fingers.

"How do you know I was troubled by the latrine?" I asked.

"It's my living," he said casually. "I go about villages removing carcasses from folks' backyards. The stink and cluster of flies turn their stomachs; they summon me. They think it's some stray dog but it's mostly a wild animal."

"What is an ocelot?" I asked stupidly.

He reached out his hand. "Harris is my name," he said.

I had no choice but to shake his hand and invite him in.

"Some water will do," he said, sitting down and stretching out his legs. I poured him a cup mixed with lime and sugar. Between sips he explained, with great fluency, the ways of ocelots. "You are lucky man," he concluded. "Normally it is some other animal, sick or wounded, that emerges from the bush, lies down in tall grass and dies."

Like all yards, mine had tall grass at the sides and at the back of the latrine for the sake of privacy.

"Ocelot is money, few leave the bush, so you are lucky it chose your place. Black and gold fur. Folk pay good money to make it mat or house decoration."

I was at a loss how to respond. Was he a crook wanting money from me? "How do you know it's a dead ocelot and not my latrine? " I asked. "You have not even seen my backyard."

He looked at me with wise eyes. "I don't like to see dead wild animals. That's why I started making a living from digging graves for them." He laughed at his own folly. "Graves, yes. Folk say, just dump them in the waste ground but I've lived in the jungle most of my life. I am partly one of them. It's just me, the way I stay. Like you, I too want a grave. What do you say?"

I had nothing to say. I was glad when he sprang to his feet and went to the back door leading to the yard.

"Wait here," he said, rolling up a trouser-leg to retrieve a suspiciously sharp knife strapped to his shin. "You look like a delicate man, Mr Chinese, you don't want to witness what I have to do."

I stood at the doorway watching him move to the tall grass. The smell of rotting flesh drove me to close the door and retreat to the far end of the house. An hour passed.

"Here it is," he beamed at the door, offering me the pelt still dripping with blood.

"No, no, you keep it," I said faintly.

"But it's yours," he said.

"I insist."

"Alright then, but I don't want you to think I passed by to profit from you."

"No, no," I assured him, giving him permission to hang the pelt on the fence to dry.

"I will come back in a week to collect it. Fine if you change your mind when you see it all dry, scraped of blood stains and softened with coconut oil." He looked around for a bucket to wash his hands but I led him into the bathroom. He emerged smelling of carbolic. I made him some tea for his efforts. In truth, I wanted him to stay awhile, to feed my curiosity.

"How did you know it was an ocelot you smelled from afar and not some other animal?" I asked.

"I done tell you that I lived long in the jungle. I can tell the smell of a dead rabbit from a dead armadillo from a dead opossum. In life they have their own traits, and so in death. Folks say I have the snout of a peccary." He shuddered at the thought.

I looked confused.

"Peccary is bush pig. Ugly. They smell so bad you want to move miles, even move country! But God make them so; you can't blame them."

I stirred more honey in his tea, wanting to hear more. He

sensed my interest and chuckled. "Mr Chinese, like you want me to tutor you in our ways?"

I nodded instinctively. I had grown up in a town. The forest nearby was sparse, most trees felled to build houses. Famine was regular, all the wild animals eaten out. The only wild animals I remember seeing were stump-tailed macaques, the stars of a travelling circus. They were trained to perform. One day the circus workers butchered a female for its flesh. Her male mate was so wretched that he refused to somersault, so it was the pot for him too.

"Peccary and me part company, not so much from the smell they give off from their rump, but because they hunt in packs. They like each other's company, I like my own. Peccary is Demerara self. They sniff each others' privates, rub against trees to mark their space, their snouts trumpeting greed. In Demerara, Coolieman, Blackman, Buckman, Putagee, Whiteman, Chinaman, they make their own tribes, mark territory, keep to themselves." He paused for me to pose another question, but before I could he continued, "I just wander, that is me. Jungle, town, village, wherever my mind takes me."

"How do you feed your body? How do you buy things?"

"In the jungle, so many cashew nuts, so many fruits fall in the ground, but be careful! Only eat what birds peck, the rest are poisonous, especially berries. They look bright and tempting on the ground, like gemstones. Take one bite and your mouth burn, your throat swell, breath stop."

"A man cannot live by berries alone. You must have some skill that you market."

"I don't have skills, only my own ways, and I get by. Didn't you just give me a rich pelt? What need for money except for a few clothes. Food plenty, pepper on every tree. You can make your own salt easy. What day you take for rest, or do Chinese not keep a sabbath?" I felt shamed by his question. Every day me and my stock kept tight company, whereas he was free to stray.

"Sunday," I lied.

"Alright, I will come back on Sunday. An outing for you. Not far, a place where fish plenty."

★

95

Sunday came. Early morning Harris was there with a donkey and a cart.

"I buy it," he said, a hint of pride in his voice.

"How much?" I asked automatically. "Where did you get money?"

"I buy it to serve you. The ocelot pelt and thirty dollars will do. I done negotiate."

"But, Harris, you can't afford a donkey and cart. Look how flat your pockets are. In fact your pants don't even have pockets!"

"I like my pants so. Why do I need pockets when I don't want anything to put in them? I buy the donkey and cart on trust, till month end, then you will need to pay the thirty dollars."

I was dumbfounded and felt anger searing my throat. "Harris, you have no right – "

He interrupted me, putting his hands together as if intending to pray. "The heat will kill you out," he said. "Bicycle cheaper but the road rickety. One day you'll break your neck." He explained he had spied my bicycle tied to the house pillar. He had witnessed the many bundles of cloth in my house. He figured out that I sold my cloth by navigating the treacherous road leading to the villages. My anger waned. Once more I felt ashamed. He was the very first native to show concern for me. For all their courtesy, my relationship with the villagers was that of seller and buyer. My small acts of charity in donating offcuts didn't alter the fact we were doing commerce.

"Where are you taking me this morning?" I asked as I climbed onto the cart.

"To the backdam canal," he answered cheerfully. "Full of fish. I'll teach you how to feed yourself."

A clucking and tug on the reins and we were off. It was a difficult ride; rain had fallen overnight and the sun had not yet sucked up the puddles. The donkey groaned as it dragged the cart along. Harris occasionally jumped down.

"Hold the reins," he said, pushing from behind with all his might to overcome a pothole spilling over with red mud like an open sore. He sought to entertain me as we resumed the journey, to distract me from my discomfort. "Over there," he said, pointing to a clump of trees, "they bear jamoon. You ever taste?"

I didn't recognise the name of the fruit.

"Don't eat jamoon when you go selling; they stain your teeth purple. Folk will believe your gums are bleeding and shun you for having rotten breath. If you try talking to them they will turn away their faces."

"You mean to say they never eat jamoon?" I asked, knowing that he was teasing me.

"Anyway, in your business you use few words. You don't talk more than two or three at a time. 'Two dollars a yard'; 'Cheap-cheap but top quality'; 'Cash, no trust'." He pointed to another tree but before he could, I identified it as tamarind. I recognised mango too. Still he persisted, calling out the different trees, until we reached the canal. Sensing that I was not overimpressed by his knowledge – I rarely relished local fruits, oversweetened by the tropical sun, apart from bananas which had grown plentifully in my parents' plot – he offered to tutor me on fish.

"Let us walk along the canal till we reach the right spot. More fleshy fish there. Here is only minnows. I can tell from the bubbles they make in the water. Different fish make different bubbles." This claim seized my attention. Up to then, during his naming of trees, I kept wondering whether Harris was a scamp. Had he planted a dead ocelot in my yard to tempt me with the prize of its pelt? What was his motive in befriending me? Theft, in all likelihood, but anything more dangerous? The local Anglican church paper carried news of a recent spate of crimes, normal ones like burglary and theft of livestock, but some too dark to commit to words. Apparently, some victims were put under a spell – everyone here believes in spirits and according to the paper they easily fall prey to spells cast upon them – and once trapped in mind, they are put to mindless acts, not so much to make money for their captor, but to turn them into slaves, totally doing whatever was demanded of them.

"Can you really tell one kind of fish from another?" I asked, caught between doubt and marvel. He smiled in pity at my ignorance.

"I'll show you," he said, reaching a bend in the canal, baiting his line and flinging it into the water with such force that I thought it would dislodge the worm. It did and Harris had to pull the line back to feed the bent needle again, which served as fish hook. He didn't seem embarrassed by this, lowering the line into the water and letting the ripples carry the bait further out. The sun was coming out strongly, so I opened my umbrella and squatted beside Harris, waiting for him to catch something. Nothing bit. He retrieved the line, put a new worm on, fatter. Still nothing. Time dragged on. Harris looked unconcerned.

"Tilapia here for sure. Bubbles don't lie. Tilapia make four-five blue-green bubbles." He was about to explain more about the different breathing of different fish when the cork dipped. Harris instinctively whipped the rod into the air. Nothing. The worm was still there. He wiped his brow, began again.

After half an hour, bored at staring at the water, I suggested going elsewhere. I expected him to feel foolish, given his boasting, but he quietly rested the rod on the ground.

"Tilapia can't master me. Wait and see!" The calmness of his voice hid malice. For all his talk of loving living things, he was determined to snare his prey. "Stay here; I will come back."

He strode off a fair distance. I was alone on the canal bank. Fearful of some wild animal coming to drink, I retreated to the cart, regretting it was not higher off the ground. I was glad for the company of the donkey. We could always leave Harris behind and head home. I could make some excuse to him afterwards, give him a dollar to make peace.

Harris returned with a bundle of leaves and stems.

"Come, Mr Chinese, come," he called. I helped him strip the stems of leaves. "Haiwa bush this," he said, prising a large stone from the earth and beating the stems into a pulp. He crushed the leaves and threw the lot into the water. Before long, four fat fish floated to the surface and drifted towards us. Harris allowed himself a smile of triumph. I was terrified. If fish can be stunned by haiwa, what about folk? Was haiwa or its cousin shrubs the means of making slaves of folk? When we reached home I prepared tea. I gave Harris all the dollars he needed to purchase the donkey and cart. Why, I don't know. The money seemed tempted out of my hands.

"You can ride donkey cart?" Harris asked. I said no. "So why did you plot to leave me behind? Donkey is danger; it could easily kill you!" He explained how a donkey could cunningly guide the cart onto uneven ground to spill its contents to lighten its load and even topple the driver. "Everything has mood. You have to sense the mood. Fish have mood. They avoid bait, out of mood, however hungry they are. That's why I didn't catch anything today."

I nodded in agreement, though not believing what he said.

"For your own sake, I'll ferry you from now on." Without waiting for my response he gulped down the tea and left. "I'll start tomorrow. Pay me in pants, if money scant." And that was that. I was hitched to Harris for all the time I spent in Demerara.

★

Another day, a few weeks into his service with me, Harris said, "Mr Jia Lun, let us take a walk in the bush. Afterwards you will fear no man."

I didn't understand so I stayed quiet.

He insisted. "Not until you spend a while in the bush can you become a true native." (Coolie Gurr was to tell me, showing off his garden, that I would only belong when I could name the flowers… a much happier prospect, and the scent of crotons, canna lilies and mimosas provoked images of you, Sweet Li Jie…).

Our first outing, to catch fish in the canal, had been a failure, and Harris had to use crushed roots and leaves to stun them. To make up for this and gain my respect, he now offered me the jungle in which he claimed to have lived for many years.

"Not to pan for gold or dive for diamond, just to be. Know how to be, how to learn which berries are lush with poison, which wild beast to hide from."

Poisoned berries! Wild beasts! I broke my silence right away, declining his offer, yet hoping not to cause offence.

He tilted his head back and chuckled. "It's true, I ask too much. Chinee folk I meet don't adventure. They lock up shop when night come and wait for daybreak to open up."

We hired a purpleheart canoe and paddled along the river, a pleasant journey, the sun beaming on the ripples like gold bangles on an Indian woman's arm. We passed huge red ants' nests on the riverbank, like mounds of red gold. The bamboo grove was a palace of gold. Macaws flew overhead in loyal pairs, sporting their shiny yellow breasts. Gold everywhere and yet nowhere. Demerara was the place the old adventurers from England called El Dorado, but no one ever found the City of Gold. Hundreds were still combing the jungle in search of El Dorado but having to settle for sieving for grains and tiny nuggets by the riverside.

We passed a cow pasture full of kiskadees and gauldings; Caribs' huts with kerosene lamps hanging from the rafters; men outside grating cassava; women, some in bead aprons, beating clothes on the riverbank or scrubbing pots with shreds of coconut husk; thatched houseboats ferrying cashews and melons from one village to another. Harris, knowing that I was captive in the canoe, tried to scare me with talk of river demons but I brushed him aside with a compliment.

"I am with you, no harm will befall me," I said. I stared at the grove of golden bamboo which reminded me of home and of you, Sweet Li Jie. Fright only gripped me when we moored, wading through mud (tiny crabs scooted into the safety of their holes as we approached) and entered the jungle through a parting of bush. A stretch of slushy mud greeted us. Harris strode ahead. I was fearful of slipping.

"Slow down, Mr Harris, why you hurrying?"

He looked back at me and smiled.

"So what if you fall? You can wash in the river. Sun will dry you out quick-quick."

Wash in the river with its flesh-eating fish and alligators!

"Plus a lot of river snakes," he said, reading my mind. "Just steady yourself and follow me."

We walked for ten minutes or so, then I stopped him again.

"I feel tired from all the rowing; let's just go back to the canoe."

I was lying. I had looked up to see huge spiders' webs between branches. What else lurked in these trees? It was time to retreat. Ahead looked like a tangle of liana vines and shrubs, vegetation broken-minded in the cloistered heat. Harris feigned disappointment. He was of course glad of my cowardice. Back at the canoe, we unwrapped bake and saltfish and drank bush tea sweetened with wild honey, all made by Harris.

"If caiman come, just bash it with the paddle," Harris said. "Keep your hands inside when you eat."

I gave him a disapproving look. He relented. No more talk of jungle things with claws and more. No caiman came but another canoe bearing a dog and two boys. The boys greeted us before hurrying off into the jungle.

"Buck boys," Harris explained. "Hunting labba. The dog will haul labba from their holes." He went on to describe labba – a large ratlike creature – as the sweetest bush-meat. "I used to hunt but night time best to catch them, though you meet up with rattlers and green-parrot snakes when it is dark. Buck boys must be hungry to hunt in this heat. When turtle-meat short, and cassava stunted in baked earth, Buck people really punish, belly bloat, fevers and other sickness. When I lived around here, I always felt for them. But what to do? When drought come, I would go without meat. That's how I come to give up. Then again, I couldn't stand killing anymore."

We left behind the chaos of palm trees tresselled with bush-ropes and vines and took to the clear river. Harris was silent. He dipped a calabash shell in the water and sipped from it, all the while staring at the ripples breaking gently against the riverbank.

At long last he turned to me and asked, "So, who are you? And me? And we?" He swept his arm before him, gesturing to the jungle to involve it and all its creatures in his question. "Scrape off the surface of your eye so to see more, like how we scrape off tons of topsoil to get to gold, acres and acres and acres of it. Each leaf and grain of dirt we scape away is all of the surface of human beings. Like stars. Dots of light. Scrape away the clouds, the whole sky, all the darkness, then you see them clearer."

Whatever he was struggling to tell me obviously failed. He saw the stupidity on my open face refusing to be scraped off. He tried again with something homely.

"Like scaling fish to see the flesh underneath."

Mention of fish set me off! Scaling fish, scaling topsoil, scaling the sky and clouds… madness!

"Man, Harris, let's just head home safe," I said.

He glared at me as if he wanted to bellow, to blow away leaves and grains of dirt heaped upon my mind.

★

Harris paddled in silence, withdrawing into himself. I, too, was silent, reckoning the task that lay ahead for the next week. I tried to block out the sight of white cranes hemlining the sky or the parade of kingfishers – the beauty of everything reminded me of you, Sweet Li Jie. When we reached to where our donkey waited, we made our way from the river through courida, mangrove, crab grass and mud. Children, mostly naked, were sticking grass knives into the backs of crabs, then stuffing them into cloth bags. Others, armed with slingshots, were hunting gulls for their goblets, which, stretched between poles, would make drum skins. As I walked along the river bank, death lapped at my feet.

I made tea, as usual, for Harris.

"I didn't mean the jungle to frighten you," he said. "When I was young, I ran away from home to live with the Carib people, don't ask why, even I don't know. My parents had a nice farm, enough to eat and a church and school nearby. My mother used to tell me how bright I was. She used to grow my brain with fish-eggs and eddoes boiled in coconut milk – her secret and sworn recipe to nurture brightness in her boy. But the jungle has a way to lure you in. People mostly go to find gold nuggets and gemstones. I just wanted to live wild, so a Carib family took me in. They showed me how to hunt, dodge snake, which vine to chew to ward off bad spirits. I built a den high up a mora tree, and not too long I learnt how a squirrel monkey chatters differently from a spider monkey and capuchin. If you don't train your ears they're all the same." He fell silent again, no doubt remembering his youthful adventures, his schooling in the ways of the wild. But when he emerged from the tree top it was God that was on his mind. He spoke at length, and with such ardour that I feared interrupting him, fearful of bringing a curse on my head.

Harris's talk made me recall Reverend Muir, the Scottish teacher/ preacher in my hometown, who had introduced many Chinese families to Jesus, but most of us were too busy on our plots, waiting for seeds to sprout, goats to breed and fowl to lay, to bother about his book. Still, being a white man, we welcomed his presence if his god would keep drought at bay. And I happily accepted his gift of a Bible and an English dictionary.

Harris's belief in God was so complicated and meandering that it's best I list what I think he said, tallying being my nature.

1) It all began with a tiny-tiny-tiny speck in water which suddenly flicked and flicked and flicked again and came to life.

2) The speck multiplied, bundled the bits, multiplied again, then after a million years, grew feet and moved onto land.

3) The speck, now bigger and more complex, grew a stomach next, then over millions of years the stomach grew a covering of different types of fur or skin, and that was the beginning of the mouse, the rabbit, the worm, the man, the woman. The specks that stayed behind in the water became mostly fish.

4) The woman, squatting on the earth to ease her bladder, was infected by a worm. Her belly swelled and the pain was so much that she searched for a stone to bash whatever was growing in her. When she used the stone, something oozed out from her. Man was born.

5) After countless more years there were millions of women and men killing animals to eat, killing each other… Wars, famine, plunder, on and on and on, till God came in the form of Love. Love was hung at the Cross but couldn't be killed. Love stepped off the Cross, melting nails and hardness of mind.

"Which brings me to the two of us," Harris said, leaning towards me. I thought I smelled rum in his breath, but I might have imagined this. "Yes, the two of us," he insisted. "After the first speck, the first flick to now, we are becoming Love. A long way to go, yes, but we are becoming, you and me and all that moves on the earth, we are all becoming Love."

I recalled the children stabbing hapless crabs or stunning gulls as they innocently flew by. My face must have creased, for Harris anticipated my doubt. He started to explain, but I ignored him, stooping down not to worship God, but to scratch between my toes.

"A little jigger; it will come and go," he reassured me. "If you walk in mud, you are bound to catch jigger. Come, let me help you."

"No, no, it is nothing," I said, wanting him to leave, wanting to rest.

My toes swelled that night so much I couldn't sleep. The next morning I looked aghast at my peeling skin. Harris examined my set of sewing needles, selected an appropriate one and poked between my toes to find the 'speck' or sandfly which bored into my flesh to lay eggs down the sides of my toenails.

"So the worm which infected me with jigger is still far away from the state of Love?" I asked. I should have kept my mouth shut instead of mocking him, for it only set him off again.

"We are men," he said. "Once upon a time we were less than worms, but now we make medicine, music and what not."

He poured rum over the blisters which stung and provoked me to taunt him again. "This sandfly will take too long to learn flute and 'what not'. Just murder it now!"

All living things were evolving towards 'Love', he told me. He had read in the local newspaper about a genius called Darwin who was trained in how to stuff birds by a Demerara black man, who had somehow ended up in Scotland where Darwin lived. Once these birds' stomachs – one of the earliest deeds of creation – were removed, the scientist could better study beak, feather and what not. "Stomachs don't tell you much, they are the basics. Thank God for that black man who cleared the way for understanding the secrets of God's mind!" He dug again, poured more rum. I would have laughed but for the pain.

★

Dear Sweet Li Jie, four days of lost sales – more distressing than jigger – for it took me that long to be comfortable on my feet again. Harris came to the house every morning to make sure I was healing. He didn't divulge any more about the secret of God's mind, sensing that I was brooding over my bales. On the fifth day we loaded a few onto the donkey cart and set off to our selling spot. Strange that we saw no-one as we trundled along the dirt-road. Even Coolie Gurr was not in his garden, and not a dog in sight. Harris rang the bell till his wrists hurt, but no one emerged. He took to the conch. Eventually an old woman pushed aside her door-cloth, poked her head out and shouted at us to go away.

"Gwan, gwan! Bell will bring more bacoo, haul you rass!"

Such a shrill outburst from her aged mouth surprised me. Harris went to her and they whispered to each other. When he came back, he told me that two young girls – sisters – had gone missing. One of the nastiest of spirits – bacoo – was to blame for the girls' disappearance.

"Best we go. No one will come out. They'll hide in their houses for as long as it takes," Harris explained.

"A day or two?" I asked.

"For as long as it takes," he repeated, his face pale with horror. "When the girls come back or police fish them out from the canal, then we can sell. Nobody will buy now, especially cloth which reminds them of winding-sheets. Stock up on rice, flour, chickpeas and business will boom."

A constable from Gladstone Town eventually showed up on his horse, about two days later. He scribbled in his notebook so furiously that the pencil point broke. Satisfied that he had showed effort and fulfilled his duty, he rode away. Folk waited in vain for his return. A week passed. Folk began to resume their ordinary lives, but still they did not buy cloth. They had protected their houses with offerings to the bacoo of rice, flour and chickpeas left at doorways.

"I should have heeded you," I said, looking sadly at my unsold cloth.

Harris frowned at me, tutting in disbelief. "You mean to say you were really thinking of making a killing selling foodstuff for bacoo?"

I had mistaken his black joke for sound business advice. Yes, Sweet Li Jie, I felt heartless, sick of myself! My loneliness in Gladstone Town was making a miser of me. When folk only have themselves, they shrink the world to pocket-size. How badly had I let down Master Yu Hao! I was so full of shame that I could not look Harris in the eyes, much less speak to him. I decided to pack up, move to another town, maybe leave Demerara altogether. A year had passed and I had done nothing but make money and shrink the world to pocket-size. Between Coolie Gurr and Harris, I had learnt much about Demerara ways, their gods, their goods, but nothing really moved me. I just longed to go home! Harris – expert on moods – sensed my thoughts.

"How many times I told you to mix with your mattie Chinese if only to exercise your tongue? Don't you miss the way Chinese words sound, or do you just talk to yourself in front of a mirror to give you grounding? Tell me that at least you dream in Chinese, otherwise you are a lost man! Tomorrow, let me ferry

you to Longping's den – the place flowing with talk... And more,"
he added, a glitter in his eye.

★

Dear Sweet Li Jie, I write this to myself, not for your eyes, about
my visit to Longping's gambling den, so when I return to Wuhan
I will go over all my writings... reminisce, regret.

There was more cursing than talk! A hut hidden from sight
in the shadow of tamarind trees, and a dozen Guandong men
squatting, throwing dice, sucking on opium pipes, slapping
their thighs in disgust or joy, their fingers drumming the
ground like palpitating birds as the dice rolled. I squatted beside
them, not to gamble, but because the fumes concentrated in the
enclosed space made me dizzy. No one bothered to greet me. All
were in frenzy or intense focus on the dice tumbling along the
floor.

A woman – the only one awake in the den, two or three
sprawled out in hammocks – came up and squatted beside me.
She had sloping shoulders, slanting eyebrows and the almond-
shaped eyes of a phoenix.

"Here, eat this," she said, offering me a five-finger fruit. I was
taken aback by her kindness and took the fruit. "It will bring luck.
Bite into it, then put down your money."

Of course I hesitated, I had no intention whatsoever to part
with my money.

"You don't trust me or what? You think I will fool you?" she
asked. She unbuttoned her blouse to expose her neck and shoulders, which shone like marble.

I mumbled something polite, telling her I was not a gambling
man.

She looked at me in contempt or disbelief or both. "Eh, eh!
And you is fellow Chinese?" She leaned towards me and whispered, "Is something else you want?"

I noticed her lively black eyes, soft fleshy mouth. She smelt of
sweat sweetened by opium fumes. A thing of devilish prettiness.
I looked down, to deny her, only to notice her anklets of grey buck
beads, thinly threaded to invite easy rupture. I looked up, dwelling on her kingfisher-blue crepe dress patterned with flowers. I
wondered where she had bought the cloth, how much she paid,

as a way of distraction. She snatched the fruit from me as suddenly as she had given it.

"Is peri peri pepper you want, not five-finger? Is not luck you want is hot-hot fuck?"

The question made me cringe. I looked out of the window to see two scarlet ibises pecking at the earth, their necks curved like question marks. That I was surrounded by men and their vile outbursts had little effect on me. Only her invitation. I noticed again how soft and fleshy her mouth was. It would have been suitable for one of Dr Richmond's drawings of naked women, except that Dr Richmond's bodies were headless.

"Men have loved me. Many wanted marriage and family. I am not only what I seem," she said, turning away her face as soon as she spoke. It was as if she regretted her vulgarity, and knowing that I was a good man, neither gambler nor opium addict, she wanted to elicit respect from me. I could have, with a gentle palm, turned her face to me, so I could peer into her pure and bewildered eyes, but I was too shy. When I left, I offered her a sum, enough to feed her addiction, but she just stared at my tainted hand and said nothing.

I hid her peri-peri proposition from Harris who inquired after my experience of the den.

"You lose to dice or to Pigeon-tail, the new girl?" he asked, grinning at me. "Yes, she took up shelter in the den only a month ago, but I hear she's learning quick. Given time, she'll be a chewed-up sugar cane. Pigeon-tail, that's her call-name. Her real Chinese name nobody knows. We name her so because a pigeon in flight opens up its back wings, spreads them wide to catch the breeze. Yes, she's more addictive than opium. Men cower at her feet, beg for favours, since she is fresh. She favour you? They say she can bend and contort and somersault like a circus star."

Guilt clouded my eyes. "I have Sweet Li Jie. I am promised to her, I have no other need. Plus she says she is not what she seems, or what she will become if she stays in the den. Who knows what brought her to a tenancy in that place?"

The months spent in Demerara had accustomed me to vulgarities, but I was taken aback by Harris, that he (a thinking man with an air of mystery) should speak so commonly, in so grossly a down-to-earth way about a woman. Perhaps he was trying to shock me. All my time with him meant facing challenges. He set out to move me sideways, upwards, downwards, any direction but the one I settled for – beside my comforting rolls of cloth.

★

Sweet Li Jie, the drama of the gambling den was a disturbance to my daily routine, and I wished for no more such. I will not go on about this, too taxing experience.

Thankfully, expectations of tragedy ended when the sisters, supposedly abducted by the bacoo, most evil of spirits, returned to their village in one piece. I could have easily gotten the story of their disappearance and return – their adventures over the two weeks interval – but I forbade Harris to speak any more of it. He had started to tell me that the girls, perhaps lured by promises or by tales of the city, had been found in a Georgetown place of ill repute.

"How and why they got there, and what they did, or what was done to them, is not my business," I told Harris, turning my back on him. "I'm just glad to know they are alive." I was sure it would be a saga peppered with lewd details, involving blackmail, kidnapping, spells, beatings and the rest, and I would be overcome with sadness. Better not to know.

Trade resumed, the villagers themselves behaved as if nothing had happened, no doubt out of shame or to protect the reputation of the sisters.

CHAPTER TWO
Meeting Coolie Gurr

Dear Sweet Li Jie, it was one month-end when I met Gurr. Some of the villagers had made good their month-end promises of payment, and even started to address me as Mr Jia Yun. They were beginning to appreciate that I never pressed them for money and, indeed, would reduce their debt depending on their distress. Before, they just hailed me as 'Chinee' or as 'Chung' (I suspect because it rhymed with dog-dung) or 'Chin' (because it rhymed with dustbin). I didn't really mind the veiled insults – that as a Chinese I preyed on stray dogs. And, in truth, their address was not spiteful, for they gave each other nicknames. A boy deprived of milk as a baby, which caused his limbs to curve, they called 'Bowfoot'. They identified each other by obvious features or ailments. 'Bruk foot' (a man with a limp), 'Big Toe' (someone with huge feet), 'Aunty man' (a man with the soft voice and manners of a woman), 'Black jumbie' (a particularly dark-skinned fellow). My favourite was an Indian coolie called 'Gurr'.

"Me name Gurr," he told me as he looked for a pleasing colour for a shirt. "Them call me 'Gurr' from since I small."

I thought immediately of Reverend Muir, the Scottish pastor who'd been our schoolmaster. Perhaps Gurr had a trace of white blood in him, some Scotsman interfering with his female fore-bears. I looked closely at Gurr to discern any trace of Scottishness (the schoolmaster had an outsized nose and red hair) when he leant aggressively towards me and bellowed, "It's short for gorilla." He burst out laughing, pointing to his forehead and the whole of his face. "You see how flat my nose and forehead is? And balloon for nose-hole? You see how ugly I look? I is a true-true gorilla. From since I born, folk take one look at me and give me that call-name."

He seemed pleased by his apelike appearance, secretly proud of himself. It marked him out, made him a recognised figure, even though of lowly status. I felt obliged to admire him, so I stared at his face, as opposed to the coins he was putting in my hand.

'Gurr' turned out to be an apt call-name. He was a gentle creature, harmful to no-one. He kept two dogs in his yard, letting them roam freely. He kept them not as guard dogs (the villagers hardly had anything to steal) but for the sake of their company. Oftentimes, as I passed his yard on my way to the selling-spot, I would see him feeding his dogs with leftover food from his pot, mostly fish he had caught in the backdam canal. The clay stove was braced against the outside mud wall and brushwood crackled and smoked beneath the pot. "Unless I hungry bad I'll always leave something in the pot for my dogs," he told me. He had hailed my cart and invited me into his yard for some coconut water. As I pushed open the gate, the dogs rushed to me, prancing at my feet or lifting their heads to lick my hands. "They don't bite. God make them special so. No matter if you throw stone at them or starve them, they stay just so."

"No doubt they take after you then," I said, as a way of showing friendship. It was uncommon for native people to invite you to their house but Gurr did so. I used to think it was because they were suspicious of what was foreign, which is what I was as a Chinaman. But when I looked around at the bareness of Gurr's home, I realised it was because they were shy of exposing their condition to outsiders. They had so little – a few pots, calabash shells to drink from, a mud cooking stove, coconut shells for fuel, rice bags for bedsheets, oil lamps – but such want was common to all of them. I wanted to think that their best belongings were each other.

"Thank you, Mr Gurr. The coconut water was just what I needed."

"Sun hot-hot. I glad," he said, splitting the coconut into two and carving a spoon from the shell for me to eat the jelly. "But, man, don't call me 'Mister'; it not nice. Gurr will do. 'Mister' is so..." He paused, rubbed his tongue along his gums and spat out a morsel of an earlier meal. He seemed to think for a while about what he intended to say. "I don't mean you bad, but 'Mister' is for them big white folk. Ride horseback with whip in hand, then you are a 'Mister'. We is small people, we born to cut cane and dig jigger from we foot. In a next life I might be 'Mister', but for now I just want to get by and to keep a clean house and nice up the place with flowers."

I looked around the flower beds he had lavished such care on, one with frangipani, others lilies, orchids and more. His house was too frail to be propped up on stilts to survive flooding, but he had made a raised crust of cow-dung at the doorway to stop rainwater.

"Wife-job, but I get no wife, how I ugly, so I do all myself. Plaster new mud on the wall, cut new grass for the roof. Here, let me show you the flowers. You is Chinee. Them things don't grow in your country. Is only when you know all the flowers and their names – what grow where, when to water what and how much, what mixture of dung to nourish the roots, how to protect them from snail and slime – that you become local. The what, the how and the where, because some will want part-shade, some will want full sun."

He gave me a tour of his garden, pointing at which bloom was ideal to seduce butterflies or hummingbirds to adorn the yard. "You'll be a true local, you will stop being foreign when you plant. Wait, wait, wait from seed to sapling, to shrub to flower, long-long, and all the time you feeding the roots, plucking dead leaves, watching with pride the stem grow straight, tall. Is a secret pleasure that make you feel more worth than being only a canecutter. And how your heart wail when rain come too plenty, and you wake up and see your plants wash away! Or when goat stray in your yard and eat them out. What to do? What to do?" He withdrew within himself as if remembering some former ruin of his garden, though I suspect it was human ruin which brought him to his lonely condition. He sensed my question and sought to bond with me by confession. "Is wife-job for true, planting flowers. Flowers like pickni, and pickni is wife-business. No wife, no pickni, but frangipani and dog keep my company. I live for my garden, I have flowers, I am not in want… Yes, is true I does wish for more…"

★

Dear Sweet Li Jie, I cannot go to the villages without stopping at Gurr's yard to drink coconut water. It has become a compulsion. Harris stays by himself, feeding the donkey or merely sitting at the back of the cart staring into space. Harris is a tall slender man, smooth-faced though in his fifties, light-skinned, tiny glittering eyes, reminding me of my needles – unlike Gurr, who is short, hairy, and molasses dark. Gurr is wide-eyed and wide-mouthed, glad to show me or talk about anything. If Harris found comfort in solitude, Gurr was otherwise, fussing over his dogs and flowers, greeting anyone who passed his door.

"What are you selling today, Chinee?" he asked me one day. "You got anything in purple?"

"Only red, green, orange. You only like purple?"

"No, I own nothing purple. I only asked because I know you'll never have that colour and I got no money today. Or any day."

"So you're asking so as to be friendly?"

"Yes, man, you is friend. If my pocket empty, I can still give you some hope."

Hope. Harris's teaching about 'month-end' came to mind.

"My father beat manners into me. Offer, even if you have nothing, and pray you don't have to give, and that 'no thanks, another time' comes back as the reply."

"So what would have happened if I did have purple cloth?"

"Man, that is a hard one, my father never teach me that. But you don't have purple cloth, so it don't matter."

"Yes, but what if I had?"

"If you had?" He wiped some coconut jelly from his mouth to speak better. "'If you had' is what bring my father and mother to Demerara. They live their years by 'if you had'. So much so that when I was born they call me *Ifwehad* because I was all they had." He stroked the head of his favourite dog, remembering his parents.

"What work did your parents do?" I ventured to ask.

"Starve. That was their last calling in India. Before that they make and market fishnets, but drought come, trench turn mud. No fish. Nobody buy fishnet. So the only thing left to do is starve."

I expected his voice to falter, but he leaned his head back to catch the sun and laughed so loudly that even the dogs were stilled.

"God called them to fishnet, then to starve, then to Demerara. One day, recruiter come to carry them away. Every day was a trial. Lord Krishna was their only solace. The recruiter came, assured the villagers that Demerara was already settled by Hindus and that the British would allow them time off to hold ceremonies. Temples had already been set up, and pandits had gone from India to guide the settlers. They put their thumb prints to the official paper. Before long they were in places like Plantation Gladstone. Recruiter had plenty food. They glad to ride wagon for a month through dust and animal bones. Month-end come, and there was the sea before them and the waiting ship and stories about Demerara – how it got plenty gold. And you know how coolie like gold! Bangle, hairpin, nose-ring, finger, gold!"

Over time, I learnt as much of his history as he would relate. Shiploads fleeing famine or white man's fury. Women fleeing the shame of widowhood, the death of their husbands turning them into nothing in the eyes of villagers, even their own families! Low-caste chamar folk fleeing from beatings from top-caste Brahmins. They would go anywhere, far or near. To stay was to burrow for roots, or to borrow money to buy food, but the moneylenders' charges were so high – making you pledge land, house, wife, young daughters – so that it was cheaper to starve, to outwait the sun. Rain did come, in the person of the recruiter, who wanted nothing but little favours from the prettiest wives. "That is how I come to born, I not ashamed to say. My Pa lolo shrivel, but recruiter eat plenty, his lolo stiff and eager for woman." He went on to divulge without pause the situation of his parents; how his father, in return for a little money, accepted that the recruiter had impregnated his wife, and was glad to leave the village for Demerara. He never slept with her again since he would not eat 'juta' (apparently a Hindu practice of never partaking of food left on anyone else's plate, deeming it to be tainted). She, in turn, resented being soiled by the recruiter with her husband's consent. She was determined never to sleep with him again. Gurr was born soon after the landing in Demerara, a child so dark-skinned and apelike in appearance that his father was convinced that Lord Krishna had put a curse on them. His mother thought he resembled the recruiter and vomited at the birth, just as she had after the recruiter had dismounted from her. When baby Gurr sobbed and wailed and sought out her nipples, she remembered the wild noises the recruiter made, and his toothless gums.

Even the village midwife hurried from the scene when Gurr was born. They did not bother to call the pundit to perform the customary ceremony. They did not invite neighbours to eat 'seven curry' (made from seven vegetables and served up on water lily leaves). Thus Gurr (*Ifwehad*) received no gifts.

"Not one rass bother to bless me when I born," he said in a matter-of-fact tone. "Folk take one look at me and right away know me is bastard, me not resemble my pa at all."

In his first two years he was hidden away in the house, but he learnt to walk. When his father went to work in the plantation's punt-gang or rat-poison gang, and when his mother went to the canal to fetch water, Gurr would venture outside the hut and frolic in the vegetable garden. The purple sheen of aubergines, the feel of carilla studs, the smell of ripe peppers – these distracted him from his loneliness. No neighbours' children to play with, he said. It was the beginning of his fascination with and romance with the garden.

"I never like fruit, only coconut. There was a mango tree in the yard. I used to wonder whether my Pa and Ma break my legs to stop me leave the hut, but it was the mango tree. There it was, coloured with fruit, tempting me to climb. Mangoes smiling from a tree. Ma and Pa far. I climb it. Nasty tree! It hide a beehive so crafty that I didn't see it. The bees wait for me to stretch out my hand for a mango. The tree sway deliberate to stir them. I swear there was no breeze before. The bees fly to my face, put one sting on me! I tumble from the tree, break both legs. I limp ever since. I used to wonder whether Pa or Ma break my legs out of spite or to hide me away, and if jaguar prowl the village, then I will get catch and eat since I can't run. But it was the mango tree.

"For years and years until I turn into a man, I suspect my pa and ma for the wickedness of my broken legs, but one day a man call Kukrit (they call him so because he had a pointy head like kukrit

114

seed) meet me and tell me he see when I fall and how the bees shroud my face in black. Kukrit said, 'It's true, blacker than even you! You turn black-black. And you foot bruk. I see it. I was hurrying to market to sell plantain. I was going to stop the cart, to see how you doing on the ground, but I was late, so I just left you there. I think to myself, somebody else would come along and help. Let me go and sell before market close. I come back now specially, thirty years later, to say sorry!'"

Dear Sweet Li Jie, Gurr told me all this. He is such a storyteller, stamping on the ground, clasping his hands, full of gestures, pauses, sighs, harrumphs, acting out his story. I am spellbound. He told me how soon after his fall from the tree, Kukrit was transferred to another plantation across the river where he worked happily and provided well for his family. But karma came to him suddenly. He was cutting cane when he chopped a snake hiding between weeds. He dropped his cutlass, shocked by his act, because in one of his incarnations Lord Vishnu was a snake. He had wounded a god. He took a while to catch himself. The work had to carry on. He picked up his cutlass and leant in towards the cane to cut it, but the snake, though beheaded, still wriggled its tail. Surprised, the cutlass slipped from his hand and cut his foot. His blood fell upon the snake. Kukrit's fellow canecutters rushed to his aid, bandaged his foot by slicing strips from the cane, dropped him onto a mule cart and took him to the plantation hospital. It was during the stitching of the wound that he remembered Gurr: Gurr fallen in the mud trying to brush off and wriggle away from the bees clustered on his face. This opened up such a gash in Kukrit's mind that he became a changed man. He returned to work but was mostly silent before the cane. He no longer cursed the rumshop owner for diluting the rum, or cursed the overseer and threaten to waylay his wife, or cursed the manager in his big house for taking advantage of his girl-servants. All canecutters curse from the moment they are unloaded in the cane field from mule carts to the moment the sun goes down and work is done. All kinds of curses. They vie with each other to come up with ever more vulgar expressions – their way of coping with the heat, the mud, the rats, the mosquitoes and the sheer malice of the canefield. Cursing, to fantasize about revenge.

As Gurr told me, Kukrit, once the most creative among them in coming up with phrases of abuse, was now a glum figure, haunted by the image of a fallen Gurr.

"If I did stop, fend off the bees, strap your foot with bamboo for support, then maybe plantation doctor would have set them proper, so after a while you can walk straight, not waddle like you do now," he said, a miserable penitent before Gurr. He held out a small purse. "Take it. My savings from all last year, enough to buy a donkey to help you move around."

Gurr looked at the purse – a piece of cloth tied with string – then into Kukrit's eyes, which were moist with emotion. "I don't venture far, not because of my lame foot, but my pa and ma make me get used to being in this one place," Gurr replied. "I stay content in my garden. That is enough horizon for me. But why you bother with me? Is my fault that I fall off the mango tree."

"Cause God curse me when I chop snake. I must remedy past sins and you is the biggest. Just take the money so I can make amends." Kukrit confessed that he had grown morose and solitary, making excuses not to drink and cavort with his fellow canecutters after the day's work. In bed, he turned his back on Surya Devi, his wife, and barely slept. He ate little. He could not cut as much cane as before. His weekly wage was also falling. His wife had to make do with less flour, less ghee.

Kukrit's wife was in such distress that, over their evening meal, she blurted out, "Kukrit, man, if is money you want for another woman, I don't mind. Take what I have! Sell my gold bangles!"

Kukrit was so taken aback that he nearly choked on his aloo curry. "Woman?" he spluttered. "What woman? What you saying?"

"What else is there to pine for in this place? We live like mouse on little. We can't get more. You can only dream, and man can only dream about woman," Surya Devi said, without rancour.

Kukrit was overcome with the desire to run his hands soothingly on her face. It was the same feeling he had when he first saw her in the village in India. His father's cow had been stolen and Kukrit had gone in search of it, in unfamiliar places, miles from where he lived. And there she was, with the last light of the day settled on her face, her hands busy gathering frangipani to offer to the gods before retiring to bed. He had come up behind her. She'd spun around, clutched her flowers and run away. He spent a while tracing her. He waited and waited by the frangipani bush until she appeared.

"Marry me," he blurted out, emerging from his hiding place. She ran. He followed. Her cries brought her father to the doorstep. It was a ramshackle hut, coconut branches for a roof. He knew that any proposal of marriage would be grasped by the father. After all, Kukrit's father (before the famine) had two cows and a small rice-field. Once they realised Kukrit was a devoted Hindu, able to recite from the *Ramayana*, pray often and moderate his liquor, they were happy their daughter would be his.

Years later, when Kukrit was transferred to the Rose Hall plantation in Corentyne, he was promoted to the mule-gang, less work and better wages, since the mules pulling the punts to the sugar factory were specially bred, expensive and treasured – certainly more than him. Now he had come back to Gladstone Plantation in Demerara to seek Gurr's blessing, and hand over some of the extra money he had earned and saved over the year. There was no need for his wife, Surya Devi, to sell her bangle. Now she believed him, relieved that no outside woman was involved. She encouraged him to visit Gurr and buy him a donkey.

"All afternoon Kukrit beg me to take the money, in between telling me his story," Gurr told me. "I refuse but he beg so hard and night was coming so I take the purse. I pick some bora, carilla, seime, bundle them up and give him to take to his wife. I buy a dozen paint brush with his offering."

"Paintbrush?" I asked. "You didn't tell me you are a house painter."

"Man, Chinee, I like it when you stop by my yard and I like tell you story so you can belong, but piece-piece. I can't tell you everything, otherwise you will stop coming." He suddenly looked broody, as if all his previous talk about being content in his solitude – just he and his flowers, his vegetable patch and dogs – was false. He told me he was proud to be different, proud to be a bastard, indifferent to his lameness, and the fact that none of the villagers admired him didn't matter. "From since I small they keep the girl children from my sight in case one of them stupid enough – or some bacoo spirit enter her head – to want my company. Yet I leave a mark on all of them. They beg me to come to their house, cook me curry, offer coin, but what I do for them I do for its own sake, not for food or fortune." He brightened up, relishing my confusion. "Chinee, you better go. Market waiting for you. Next time you come, I will show you."

★

Dear Sweet Li Jie, Gurr eventually let me enter his hut. Dark. Smelling of dog. A few pots and a stool with bamboo legs on the floor. He lit an oil lamp and pulled away a cloth covering the far wall. I gasped! A blaze of colours!

"Lakshmi," he said, pointing to the gold of her raiment, the gold necklaces and bangles. "She is the Hindu god of fortune." It was a gaudy painting, the gold blinding rather than provoking marvel. "Is true, I make it too bright," Gurr said, as I narrowed my eyes. "But I calm down things with her face." I looked again and indeed her face was a soft blue and the background, showing foliage, was done in pinks, pale yellows. "Stupidness really," Gurr said, telling me that Hindu deities were all unreal. "If they be true, how come Lakshmi never answer prayer? Look how the whole village hand-to-mouth. See how I rest the lathi by her feet?" He pointed to a rod – the lathi – and a piece of cloth knotted at the top to form a bundle. "It belong to my father. He fill the bundle with his few belongings, sling the lathi over his shoulder and board coolie boat bound for Demerara. It is my heirloom, the only remains of him. Me, I don't believe in Lakshmi and how she bring plenty pomp and paisa to people. I prefer to believe in dog."

"So why put Lakshmi on your wall?" I asked, now accustomed to the blast of gold and admiring the beauty of the work. He paused as if to think, then turned away and scrunched his mouth. I gazed at the painting, moved by the passion of shapes and colours. There was no need for Gurr to explain himself. The Hindu gods might be all foolishness, but he could paint them, lose himself and lose the world in the sheer happiness of daubing, stippling, getting his hands soaked in dyes, forgetting all but the need to colour, to shape.

"I make a dollar here and there," he said, telling me that the villagers at each festival would commission him to paint their cardboard or clay gods, to refresh the deities in their home shrines. "Gorilla I am in truth, but I is their god-man. I restore colour to what flake and fade, but I never believe any of the gods is real."

Whenever I visited his garden, I understood that the white, the yellow, the blue flowers – the flourish of colours – were his way of daubing the earth with living paint. Inside his hut and outside, this Coolie-man was a maker of spectacle.

★

Dear Sweet Li Jie, Gurr surprised me with his painting but also with his sudden suspicion of Harris.

"He has the green eyes of a jaguar; don't trust him," Gurr said.

I was taken aback by this outburst. "What do you mean?" I asked, looking at Harris who was, as usual, reclining in the donkey cart, peering at the clouds. Gurr muttered something too softly for me to catch.

That night sleep would not come to me. I lit a wicker torch and went outside to breathe the fresh night air. I made some bush tea to calm my nerves. The latrine at the far end of the yard gave off a sudden stink. I imagined that toads were wallowing in the waste, giving rise to the odorous waft. I resolved that the next day I would suppress the latrine stink with white lime. I distracted myself by staring at the two midnight orchids Gurr had given me. They only flower in the dark, and many a night and many a lonely time they kept me company. I would watch them in wonder and dwell on you and Ma Hongniang. Tonight, however, the stink prevailed over their perfume. I went back inside, the tea barely sipped. I lay in bed and pondered Gurr's words, which were as contrary as the country itself. On my journeys to the villages, the lotus lilies and hyacinths light up my senses. What colour they give to the trenches! But although sweetened by their perfume, the water remains a threat, harbouring alligators and snakes. The bullfrogs among the foliage make such ugly calls, thwarting the spectacle, reminding me that as a lowly Chinese – no, as a man, a Terence – I was always a serf to nature, quick-quick to spoil and disappear. All folk here were subject not only to the British, but to a greater force. The smell of fear filled my nostrils. I suddenly felt the need for the comfort that company brings.

So what did Gurr mean? Was he warning me that Harris would, for some reason, or no reason, suddenly or after biding his time, pounce on me like a canal or jungle creature? Was it evidence of racial feeling, given how tribal the people were, the British cunningly separating the Coolies from the Congoes from the Bucks, encouraging them to suspect each other so as the better to rule over them? I have come across gentle folk who would readily curse one another out of racial spite. I could barely follow the creole talk, but the tone of voice, the grimace, the spitting on the ground, suggested vile words and thoughts.

Or was it a matter of colour? Gurr is as black as burnt sugar, whereas Harris is light-skinned. The Colony is obsessed with colour. Gurr has explained to me that the Madrassi Coolies were equally as dark as any of the African Congoes, so were looked down upon by light-skinned folk of all races. The native Carib bush people they call 'Bucks' are like our Chinese in colour, closer to white, so they shouldn't get the same kind of abuse. But everybody deems them to be half-naked bipeds, undeserving of their pale skins.

What stupidness (or 'chups', as Harris would say)! I will happily continue to sell my cloth to all colours and leave them to their plight. Pondering on Gurr's warning tired me out. I fell asleep to the sound of rainfrogs serenading the moon.

★

Dear Sweet Li Jie, Harris keeps me alert with his banter. "You are like a saman tree watching over gravestones," Harris joked at the way I was hunched over bales of cotton, accounting for the day's dealings. "Nothing else piques your interest," he said.

"You think I should kick off my slippers and reach for a rum?" I retaliated, but with joviality, for the takings were substantial. The coolies would soon be celebrating something called Holi, where they throw dyes and splash coloured water over each other. Clothes would end in ruin, so those who could afford it bought replacements beforehand, since prices went up the very next day after Holi to take advantage of demand. Many cloth merchants – and I had a few rivals coming from other places – practised such wickedness, but I kept my prices constant. Those too poor to risk their already sparse garments went about naked at Holi but for a loincloth – I provided loincloths free of charge from leftover-ends from each roll. Besides, I was not worried about competition: all my rivals were Indians who, as soon as they made money, drank most of it out. They never kept enough to maintain their stock and they had to come to me for credit. I could, if I wanted, close down their businesses, but why would I want to? Folk would start calling me 'shut-shop chinee', loose their dogs or void their phlegm on me. Better to be called a saman tree in the village cemetery.

"At least I give shade to those in sleep," I teased Harris. "Or would you rather see me drunk, swearing at neighbours, banging drums, breeding unrest?"

Harris came back at me. "I was planning to buy you a chillam or two and grow the tobacco myself, but these would be wasted Holi gifts," he said.

★

I watched from afar the coolie villagers throwing red dyes over each other and squealing. Their joy, followed by rich vegetable curries, reminded me of our own festivals, the release of lanterns into the night sky, the dragon dances, the eating of steamed rice flourballs filled with bean paste. Of course, I missed the way our land looked, and many a times I would daydream that I was in a field of wild kapok, and crabapple flowers in full bloom. As a boy, I would watch lavender grass bowing all day, teaching me to curtsy. But I knew I was returning to China in two or three years, and the trees and flowers would be there to greet me and stay with me all my life. What I longed for daily was the taste of our food! A mooncake or a bowl of wonton soup would so appease my sorrow at being far from you, Sweet Li Jie.

Glutton Fu had warned me about this. At the Chinese cookshop in Georgetown, after he had packed his stomach and belched to make more space, he asked me, "What did you eat in China before you went on board, your last meal?" A question out of nowhere! "I can't remember…" I said. "Ah, but you will, wait and see. You'll tense up your mind, struggle to remember how everything did smell, steamed or fried, how everything did frolic on your tongue, tease it, burn it… I miss my food, my celery, my fennel, my lotus

121

root, my lichen." He paused to recall his Hakka delicacies. "The fruits here good, though. They have pomegranate, mango, banana, coconut. My father job was to climb barefoot and barehand high up coconut tree, day after day. As a boy I would gaze up to see him, full of wonder. He can do anything, I thought. If he slip and fall, he'll start flying midair. Once he slipped as he was coming down, not far from the ground. He only break three ribs but he started to bleed inside. I started to cry. My mother bore a hole in his body and suck out the blood with a pipe. You can't get more love, and lasting love, than that! I was crying. My mother kissed me on my mouth; I can still taste the blood, the salt." He sighed heavily. I saw his eyes redden. I suddenly saw another side of Glutton Fu. Travelling with Hakka people on the ship, I learnt they had a special place for hospitality in their culture, which they called '*Haoke*'. Every stranger had to be fed, to be offered a bed. *Haoke* had died in Glutton Fu, like everybody else in Demerara. Money had taken over, the desire for money, so he overcharged Chinese newcomers in his hotel, probably even raided their bundles. The colony had turned him, taken away his manners. And yet, some feeling remained, and maybe could turn him again towards *Haoke*. The more he remembered his father and mother (and surely, there was much more that stayed in his mind) the more he could become a child again.

★

Sweet Li Jie, I hesitated to tell you of my sickness, but I do so now, having recovered.

"Mosquitoes thick as porridge in all the villages," Harris told me. "Take a break from selling."

And soon enough, the speck of a creature Harris claimed was on its way to godliness, given time, paused its journey to settle on me. High fever, headaches, chills, heart beating by its own will, dark-coloured urine, malaria proper! Harris's speck which slid out of the water, grew a stomach and eventually became mosquito – a slight speck of an insect which, somehow, carried a hammer to beat me on my head. It was the near undoing of me, both me and my sales. For days I worsened until I grew delirious, seeing ordinary household things look stranger than the jungle creatures Harris had told me about. I had a vision that I was drinking from a gourd of creole liquor, when a terrapin appeared, with azure flakes on its shell, inching its way up the wall. Before it reached the top, it turned its head to me, breathed in and blew out bubbles. Suddenly a mosquito wielding an iron mallet landed on its shell and began to pound it until pieces fell off. Then a moth arose from a crevice in the moon, danced on my head, which was on fire with fever, before dropping into the flames. A mouse ran up to me, opened its mouth, shook its head and all its teeth fell out. This pageant of creatures made brief appearances and then were gone. I am ashamed to say only Pigeon-tail from the opium den stayed, night after night, as if betrothed to me. But I was resolute, however much she tried to tempt me, because you, Sweet Li Jie, were pledged to me by Ma Hongniang. Pigeon-tail was unspeakable in the ways she flexed her body – Dr Richmond, had he lived, would have had new material for his drawings. I myself did not know such details of a woman's body, until she appeared in delirium and dream.

Harris spent two weeks looking after me. He was all hours by my bedside, wetting my lips to stop them flaking. He patted me down with a lime extract mixed with alcohol – a concoction he learnt from the Carib people, he told me afterwards – to cool my face. All kinds of herbs and bark of trees were boiled, strained, sugared and fed to me, to lower my fever. Nasty to swallow, but I was too weak to vomit. Two weeks in my company, guarding my stock of cloth, dispensing bush medicine. Only later did he tell me he had stayed throughout within earshot of me, sleeping in the yard directly below my bedroom, in the donkey cart.

Gurr was just as kind. One of his dogs dropped a puppy. He brought it to me so it could lick my face and crawl under the sheet to sleep on my stomach. It brought such relief to me, just being in close companionship with another's body. And every time I woke up briefly from my hallucinations, my nose was greeted with perfume. Gurr had placed clay pots in my room, bearing flowers from his garden (which, he told me later, were lily and hibiscus used in Hindu ceremonies to remember the dead!).

"I didn't mean you harm," he told me. "They were in bloom; it was their season."

But Gurr did something so special that I cried. I opened my

eyes to see Harris with a cloth in his hand, preparing to wipe my face, and Gurr cradling the puppy in his arms as you would an infant. He had already placed fresh flowers in the room. The aroma was so strong that I sneezed.

"Give praise to Lord Krishna, you are getting strong enough to sneeze!" he said, then looked foolish, remembering he didn't believe in deities. Harris kept silent. "Here, I brought you this," Gurr said, reaching into a cloth bag strung over his shoulder. He held up a vase to me. "Don't handle it yet, you are still weak, you might drop it."

I saw it clearly only for a brief while because my eyes filled with tears. "Sweet Li Jie," I wheezed, trying to sit upright, but falling back.

"Don't fret yourself," Gurr said, "I'll put it near you to gaze at." He brought a small table to my bedside and placed you, Sweet Li Jie, there for me to behold.

During my illness, Gurr had taken the vase with your image Ma Hongniang had given me, to remember you by. The salt air of the sea – Gladstone Town being near the Atlantic – had faded some parts of it. Gurr had restored it, his way of keeping company with me during my bedridden days and nights. The vase seemed brighter than before, which I put down to his Hindu love of colourful hues. Indeed, your face looked a little less Chinese, a little more Indian, as if Gurr was trying to make you like the Lakshmi on his mud wall. If Gurr was religious, I might speculate that his restoration was a way of converting you to Hinduism! Or maybe he was saying all of us are flesh painted on the same cracked clay.

"You like it? You like it?" he asked excitedly. I wept in response. I was a stranger to Gurr, I was a stranger to his history, to his language, to his diet, to his garden, and yet he put his skills to restoring the vase so I could remember you, Sweet Li Jie, and home, and all I left behind in China. The world has evil in it. Germs killing each other, killing humans. Humans at war with each other. If you looked up to the night sky, you see so many millions of stars packed so closely, as if struggling for space, struggling against suffocation. But maybe Harris was right. Was the ready kindness of Gurr to a stranger like me a small sign that we were moving towards a state of Love; that the killings were only setbacks to what was certain to be? But strong doubts persisted. Why malaria? Why the jigger worm? Why the cholera which carried off my Master? Questions I was not bright enough to answer – if there were answers – but all the same there was something forever in the love Gurr and Harris showed me. And I felt ashamed for the way I mistook Gurr's warning about Harris as something ugly. I had thought he was being nasty against black folk, but now, both of them by my bedside tending equally to me, I realised that Gurr was only being protective of a stranger. It was normal for some folk to take advantage of newcomers. So it would be normal (in Gurr's mind, not knowing Harris) for someone like Harris to attach himself to me, to be in a better position to pounce on me. Had I not myself suspected so? No, I was wrong. Race didn't count, it was a matter of stranger, parasite, protector.

PART FIVE

CHAPTER ONE
Jia Yun: Prospect Town

Harris was right to try to prod me out of my rigid habits. He kept telling me about the new Prospect Town, suggesting that I visit. Soon after I arrived in Demerara, he had showed me the *Demerara Chronicle* which carried news, over several issues, of the building of Prospect, such was the boon it brought to the reputation of the Chinese. The *James Moses* ship, with 200 Chinese souls, had landed in January but instead of being dispersed to various plantations, they were placed in the care of Reverend Chow, a local Chinese preacher. They were Christian converts, mostly from Xiamen, not at all well off, being small traders and artisans.

Reverend Choy, who ran a twenty-acre pig farm in George-town, crammed the Chinese in makeshift huts on this farm for a short while, to accustom them to the new climate. Happily, it was the dry season, so no one died of disease and he was able to gather his flock together in the open field where the pigs roamed, for Christian service. It was not at all discomfiting to be in the midst of pigs for, as I explained to Harris, we Chinese have minded them from the beginning of time, measuring our wealth by their numbers. If only, Sweet Li Jie, I had bought a herd of swine for you, instead of the bicycle...

Reverend Choy had about two hundred pigs on his farm. As a pastor he worked for the Demerara Anglican Missionary Society, and the pigs were all branded DAMS. Reverend Chow, though not their owner, was their steward. The *Chronicle* praised him for his work with pigs and people.

The Demerara Anglican Missionary Society appointed Rever-end Choy headman of Prospect Town, where he took his pigs and people. I am told that when he entered the allocated land to turn the sod, it was like the coming of an emperor from the Ming dynasty. A church band played, two trumpeters blew fanfares and he sat on a very high chair to witness traditional dancing and singing by Chinese ladies dressed up in elaborate costumes. Whoever sewed them must have made a fortune. Indeed, I regretted not heeding Harris's advice that I should branch out into tailoring. But I digress. Let me get back to Reverend Choy.

Wondrously, within nine months, with the ceaseless labour of black Congoe carpenters, masons, painters and so on, ninety houses were built and hundreds moved in. The church appointed a policeman to keep the peace; gambling, alcohol and opium were strictly forbidden. Two catechists manned the school class-rooms. A Chinese doctor called Shen (who, I was told by Harris, turned out to be more of a butcher than a surgeon) set up a clinic and stocked it with cotton wool and bandages to soak up spilt blood.

I visited Prospect Town though I had no interest in investing or living there, but curiosity overcame me and Harris was always harrying me to get out and about more often. The excursion to the canal to catch fish, to the jungle, and venturing into a gambling den, were sufficient for me. Snakes were everywhere, reptiles and humans. My preference was shutting up shop as soon as I could, closing the shutters, rolling down the mosquito net and lying on the bed to think of you, Sweet Li Jie. You, my cloth, my scissors, my rulers, my cotton threads… the sum of my happiness. Still, I yielded to Harris. We hired a horse and carriage for the trip. I had arrived in a dray cart, but was now leaving Gladstone Town in some style. The coach-seats were thickly cushioned, there were footstools, and you could lie back, stretch out and catch the breeze from the open windows. Harris brought plenty of mauby to drink (I had taken to this local taste) and bread rolls stuffed with crispy fish, a tolerable meal, though I didn't bother much with his bread-and-fish on the journey, since Prospect Town was bound to have Chinese cook shops.

You could only appreciate so many monkeys on tree tops and the endless greenery, so I fell into a fitful sleep. Sometimes I feigned sleep, to avoid Harris's preaching about the evolution of Speck to Godhead.

What a sight greeted me when we eventually got to Prospect Town! We halted at the top of a hill, overlooking the valley to marvel at the handiwork man was capable of. Harris's conviction about human progress started to infect me.

"A new Jerusalem!" Harris said, surveying the valley below. "The newspapers was right. It is a miracle what you Chinese can do in such a short time!"

There were many newly painted wooden houses with shining zinc roofs. Yards planted with fruit saplings, with beds for bora, carilla, pumpkin. There were pigs aplenty, feeding on boiled vegetables. Rice fields. Many acres of land growing potatoes, ginger, cocoa. The trees cleared to make way for agriculture had been put to good use to make charcoal, shingles and planks. Those additional to Prospect's needs were piled onto punts and taken by river to Georgetown.

Many hands were busy in the fields supplying the capital with rice and vegetables. Other hands were maintaining the dams, or clearing the canals of weeds. And at the heart of it all was the church with its imposing bell-tower, so that when the settlers looked up from their work, it dominated their view, reminding them of God's bounty in bringing them to this happy valley – and of their obligation to work, to donate to the salary of the police-man, the catechists and Reverend Choy, and to make donations, not just to the church in Prospect Town, but to the Anglican headquarters in Georgetown. It trained the catechists and sent them all over the colony to convert those ignorant of the Gospels, especially the first natives, the Caribs , whom Harris so revered for bringing him up in a state of naturalness. Prospect Town's produce was to be at the heart of funding this Anglican effort. Headquarters planned to expand the settlement, growing it to hold two thousand people, and to rival the capital itself in generating wealth. New fields would be created for coffee and coconut production; They would build new sawmills, and triple the numbers panning for gold.

But as I looked down upon the scene, I was suddenly seized by a sense of calamity. Why, I did not understand. Strangely, the memory of the ocelot which had wandered into my garden to die came to mind. It had been a creature robed in rich fur, its head crowned in gold, and gold streaking its body. Harris had skinned it, exposing rank flesh, rank bowels, and a chaos of cut veins.

★

Harris and I stayed in a two- storied hotel run by Reverend Choy for wealthy Chinese wanting to relocate to Prospect Town or to invest in its agriculture and manufacturing. It was a hotel very different from Glutton Fu's: soft pillows, soft mattresses, scented sheets, mosquito nets, Berbice chairs to stretch out on and be served juices, platters of fruit, freshly cooked or cured meats, puddings enough to feed all the poor in the villages I sold cloth to.

An expensive hotel. I began to question its excess, but settled my conscience by accepting that the monies spent would go back to the Church for its charitable and missionary activities. Reverend Muir, who had educated me in China, spoke of Jesus fasting or sleeping on stones. Reverend Choy's sermons, which were carried in the newspapers, focused instead on Jesus's parables of investment and on the *self-improvement* that followed. I believe that this focus on *advancement* was what birthed Prospect Town.

Reverend Choy occupied the whole of the top floor of the hotel, five rooms and a bevy of maidens attending to his wants. He was indeed the Emperor of Prospect Town in his strut, his pompous bearing, the way he looked straight ahead as he passed by, ignoring the people who paused from their work and lowered their heads in respect and awe. The procession of his entourage, his maidens dressed in saffron silk, hardly looked as if they had renounced the world, the flesh and the devil.

He sought me out and asked me to dine with him in his quarters. The invitation was not extended to Harris, but I insisted, telling him that Harris was not my servant, but my friend. His dining room was adorned with vases and paintings, and there were two shelves packed with religious texts, though I also spotted one entitled *The Art of Rearing Pigs*. Of course, the only reason he invited me to the feast – the table was furnished with dumplings, ribs and other roasts, rice dishes and an assortment of fish stews – was because he thought me a man of substance, evidenced by my occupation of two costly rooms in the hotel.

"I, too, am a man of cloth," I told him when he inquired after my business.

A look of severe disappointment crossed his face.

"Only in a manner of speaking," I hurried to reassure him as he bit uneasily into a spiced bun. I knew right away that he was worried that another Chinese pastor (me) was intending to intrude on his domain. I could hear him thinking that perhaps the Anglican bishop in Georgetown had trained up another pastor (me) to minister to the swelling population of Prospect Town. Even his maidens paused from laying down fresh plates.

"I am a cloth merchant," I said and right away the maidens resumed their activities and Reverend Choy reached for two more buns.

Harris took an instant dislike to Reverend Choy. Harris, after all, claimed to be sensitive to the nature of animals. He picked at his food. I sensed he wanted to leave but could not, out of courtesy. His conversation with Reverend Choy was deliberately not on religious matters, but on pigs, as a way of insulting him.

"I know that swine suffer from all kinds of maladies in my country." Harris paused to let the two words, 'my country' carry weight. "I am wholly ignorant of their condition in *your* country. Pray, tell me."

Reverend Choy remained serene, passing me a new napkin. Harris was too inferior a man to be bothered with.

"So, Mr Jia Lun, you come from afar with fresh eyes. Tell me, Sir, what impresses you most about Prospect Town?"

"The neatness of everything," I said.

"Indeed, I planned it myself. A congregation of square plots, a house in the middle of each, the front of the plot to be planted with flowering shrubs, the back with fruit trees. The canals skirting the ricefields were cut at a precise angle to one another. There is to be no wilderness or wildness in my estate. Have you noticed how spruce is the dress of our folk, even in their work clothes? But of course you have. You are a man of cloth!"

I promised Reverend Choy that I would spend a few days in Prospect Town with a view to making an investment.

"I have reserved the choicest plots for people of your standing, right next to the church," he said. "Before you arrive, a house can be built according to your desire. An orchard planted, a servant provided. You will not be in want of workers to wait upon you here." He beamed, puffed out his cheeks, revelling in his ability to command, to dispense. "As to the cost, let us for now not dwell on such small matters, small for a man of your substance."

★

Harris and I traversed Prospect Town looking for a spot to settle. I shunned Reverend Choy's attempt to sell me land next to the church, a kind of bribe to God to induce blessings upon me.

"I could live here," I told Harris. "I like the way the place is full of ambition."

I would build a small house, set up shop on the ground floor and engage someone from the settlement to run it. Of course, I expected to be short-changed by my employee, but I would build such loss into my budget.

We stopped at the pharmacy to buy some ointment to ward off midges and other troublesome insects. The shelves were packed with herbs and roots, the scent of which reminded me of home. Perhaps this was why I seemed to recognise the pharmacist.

"Are you from near Wang Changling's village, *The Domain of Wang Qian*?" I asked. "Your face looks familiar."

He had smiled broadly at me when I entered the shop. "Ask for anything. I will gladly make it for you," he had said. His hand had gestured to the plentiful goods, ready to cure me of any illness. Now, he retreated behind the counter and occupied himself with mixing oils and herbs.

"I feel sure we have met before," I persisted.

He continued to ignore me.

"Landlord Wang Changling," I said. "He had a servant named Baoyu, a short man with a twisted jaw; you can't forget him easily."

The pestle slipped from his hand. The mortar tipped over and spilled its contents. He looked at me and gnashed his teeth. His face was flushed with rage.

"Why? Why? I made a mistake. I was a drunk, that was all! Why do all of you continue to hound me?"

I was taken aback. I looked at Harris, but he, too, was puzzled by the outburst.

"They tied me up with rope, questioned me, lashed me. I managed to escape. There were more questions before I could board the ship. More questions throughout the sailing. And when I landed, the harbour people held me, got a translator to query my past, where I was from, why I was in Demerara. They chewed me up with questions before they let me go. The gossip spread like sandflies. Nobody would let me rent. You know how much money I had to bribe Reverend Choy before he give me consent to settle here? Just get out of my shop before I chop you!"

★

Reverend Choy, still hoping I would buy a costly plot close to the church, was happy to tell me the whole story, minus of course the matter of the bribe, which I, too, was silent on.

"A quack, to be sure, Du Fu, but a man has to make a living and my calling is to forgive him, to let him have another chance. And he is very good at ridding children of lice, so he is of some use. And every week he donates to the missionary fund, so glad as he is for the protection of Our Lord."

Quack Du Fu had fled China, Reverend Chow explained. He had poisoned a female patient, making a grievous error in mixing the wrong barks and herbs. The husband, suspecting some sexual motive, threatened to kill him. Wang Changling, not wanting trouble in his little kingdom, arranged for Quack Du Fu to escape with a trunk full of medicine.

Being a simple man, he couldn't disguise his guilt; it shrouded his face. He avoided eye contact with his shipmates. He was fidgety. He kept to himself. The captain, already suspicious of his behaviour, had questioned him before letting him board. Money passed hands.

When he landed in Demerara, his nervous behaviour caused him to be questioned again by the harbour clerk, but he eventually bribed his way through Customs.

"Someone on board must have been talking about me and my work," Reverend Choy said, smiling broadly, proud that his reputation was spreading afar. "He turned up at my office in Georgetown. Penniless. I took pity on him and loaned him two pigs to breed, to slaughter and sell, enough to buy wood to build a shop in Prospect Town. He was in a hurry to hide away here, far from constables and courts in the city. But I taught him a little of the Gospels before I sent him on his way." Reverend Choy leant back on his cushioned chair, fixing his eyes on me as if to solicit praise for his piety.

Harris, who had a natural gift of connecting with strangers found out a different story from the settlers. The pharmacy was owned by Reverend Choy and Quack Du Fu worked for him as a minion, handing over most of the takings, and surviving on next to nothing. Reverend Choy had him under his control. He was not even allowed to marry for a little pleasure and companionship. Reverend Choy wanted his dedicated service. He could not escape because Reverend Choy would create new stories of Quack Du Fu's criminality in China and send constables after him. Not just one murder, but multiple poisonings. Of course, the authorities would trust the holy Reverend and jail Quack Du Fu.

"About half the people in Prospect Town are in his grip," Harris told me. "They were foolish. They confessed their sins to him, seeking God's mercy. He wields the weapon of knowledge over them. Many working in the fields, running shops, logging or in the charcoal business are making money for him. Some resent him but the simple-minded revere him and seem happy to serve him, to live under his direction. As in China – emperor and minions – thousands of years of obedience in their blood."

I visited Quack Du Fu again, now more understanding of his plight. I apologized for questioning him the day before. He was sorry for chasing me out of his shop. I offered to pay for the mixture that he spilled and for the cracked mortar. This softened him more. No one in Prospect Town, it seemed, had been kind to him, but now I, a stranger, was showing consideration. He blurted out his pain.

"Many times I have thought to poison myself. I have the herbs to do it."

He gestured to his packed shelves in despair. I looked down at my shoes.

"Yes, to answer you, I do come from Wang Changling's village. I saw you a few times from afar, when you were visiting Sweet Li Jie. I know that like you and me they left, fleeing from soldiers. Three or four others went with them. They heard about Demerara and its gold, perhaps from you. So they came here. When it was my time to run, I, too, chose here. They sailed in a ship that left before mine, two months before."

A shaft of sunlight shot through the open window straight into my eyes. I leant on the counter to steady myself. I stopped breathing. Du Fu offered me water. I coughed it out. When I caught myself, I asked, "Are you certain? Are you certain?"

I couldn't tell whether my voice left my mouth.

CHAPTER TWO
A drowning

Dear Sweet Li Jie, I have spent long hours writing to you, I planned a hundred pages if needed, to record all my doings in Demerara. A leisurely pace, a few sentences at a time, my head clear and restful. But now, panic! The world has become a whirligig. Speed, more speed! I grow giddy, I grow faint, I must put away my pen and hurry to catch a boat to meet you. Of course, I believe you are waiting for me, and you will run up to me as I approach, with a sprig of bamboo. But where? In Georgetown or somewhere up country?

"We must go now – now," I shouted at Harris, banging on his door in the hotel. "Hire a boat. Hire a tracker."

Harris was taken aback, thinking sunstroke had shot my mind. He sat me down. He fanned me. He sprinkled cooling water on my face. When I came to my senses, I told him what Quack Du Fu had disclosed, that many villagers from different parts of my province had headed to the Colony, drawn by the stories of its plentiful gold. Many had headed to Bartica, up the Essequibo River, and thence into the jungle to pan for gold. But many then emerged from the jungle and sold the gold they sieved from the creeks to the dealer in Prospect Town, Dealer Dong Dong, before setting off for Georgetown to set up shop. Dealer Dong Dong paid a little more than they would get in Georgetown, so Prospect Town was the first place they all came to.

I sought out Dealer Dong Dong and he told me that no-one like Sweet Li Jie and her mother had brought gold to him, so I decided we had to head up river.

★

Harris hired four natives who knew the river well. They would

138

do the paddling and when we stopped they would cook for us. We would be seven days travelling, stopping at small clearings on the riverbank where groups of Caribs had erected huts. If we had to take overnight shelter, our crew would strip the trees or branches for cover and cut vines to fasten the poles.

We passed poor, half-naked people, living on fish, alligators, wild meat, cassava. The women cooked. The men hunted. They had been living so for centuries, depending on visiting missionaries for salt and sugar, and a little schooling for their children. I felt sickened, overcome by the rawness of their lives – the mud, the mosquitoes, the cockroaches, the stench of rotting vegetation and of animals being cut open. Stifling heat. Moss, lichen, liana choked the endless stretch of trees. Above all, the depression that came on me when none of the villagers knew of your whereabouts, or whether you and Ma Hongniang had ever passed their way.

Harris took pity on me. The crew cut down a tree, made a dugout and one of them paddled me back to Prospect Town.

"Stay there," Harris said. "I will carry on the search for them. The bush is not made for a city man like you."

Reverend Choy was glad to see me, not least because I would be staying longer in his hotel. He made a half-hearted attempt to ask after you and Ma Hongniang, but offering no sympathy. Instead, he appointed two of his women disciples to be my carers. They were to cook exclusively for me and attend to my laundry, for a fee. It was a ploy to tempt me and make me part with more money. One woman was particularly bold.

"Everybody says she is beautiful to look at, pale-skinned, fleshy lips, pointy chin, wild thick eyebrows which, even better, are joined," Reverend Choy had said, offering me her services.

I could not look away since she was always parading herself before me. She giggled when she spoke, as if to present herself as an innocent schoolgirl. Instead of making up my bed, cleaning the room and leaving me, she would linger and insist on talking, always about herself, as if she was selling herself, pointing out her best features. "Bid for me," she seemed to suggest. "You have to be rich enough to afford me." I had no desire to be part of Reverend Choy's marketplace. Whenever I tried to leave the room, she would hold me back with some story about her life, taxing my patience, taking advantage of my politeness.

"I was among the first Chinese women to come to the colony. The boat was packed with men, but I didn't mind their sweat, their swearing and their spitting. I had a higher purpose, to make a princess of myself. I am a pioneer. That's my name now, I answer to 'Pioneer.'" She looked me in the face, all the while twirling strands of her rich, silky hair, which reached her waist. She babbled on about the many suitors she toyed with, but then spurned, settling instead for a much older man, Dong Dong, the rich owner of a coal mine in her province, and now the gold-dealer in Prospect Town. "You might ask me why we are here now in this dismal jungle clearing," she said.

I didn't care to know. I didn't ask but she told me anyway. "The coal mine collapsed. Many died. The place became one big burial site. Families wanted compensation. My husband heard about Demerara, so he decided to open up a gold mine here. For the moment, though, we trade in gold from others who risk *their* lives doing the mining."

Another fleeing from justice, like Quack Du Fu. I wondered how many there were in Prospect Town.

★

Dear Sweet Li Jie, I no longer have any interest in Prospect Town. I keep to myself, nursing my memory of you. I continue to write, to distract myself, or I sit on the veranda staring at clouds. Sometimes I imagine they form your face. My heart beats wildly until the clouds disperse and I am left alone. The sun blisters my skin but I don't mind sitting on the veranda for hours, searching the clouds for your face, until darkness comes and the tree frogs sing the same tune all night long to torment me. A million million stars come out, crowding the sky, struggling against each other for space. I think of Harris's specks struggling to come to life, the first flick, the first movement, which in time became Man. "What happens after Man?" I once asked him, idly, concentrating more on the movement of my scissors, slicing through a piece of linen. I asked only to humour him but it was I who burst out laughing at his answer.

"Long from now we will make medicine to banish death." He

ignored my snigger. "Then we will make machines to fly to the stars. We will take over the whole of the sky. We've started already, there is now something called an airship."

There was no stopping him. I had to lay down my scissors to pay heed to his fantasy. He rambled on about how deathless Man would settle on the stars. How human bodies would change to suit their new environment, growing longer than a mora tree or with wings like a bat or maybe many eyes like a tarantula. Others would get rid of their bodies altogether, and only Thought would remain. God had created Matter, which was in its nature subject to sin and corruption, but Matter was steadily becoming Love. Love was growing within flesh, within Matter.

"I can't wait to become a super bat, a super spider or just air," I'd said, returning to cutting cloth. "Until then, prepare the donkey cart for selling."

★

Dear Sweet Li Jie, what happens when we die? I think we just die, that is all. We are not the future Harris dreams of. So I am maddened thinking that you may no longer be. I am still awaiting Harris's return. Pioneer keeps tormenting me. Today she wore a low- cut blouse. She cooed as she smoothed my bedsheet, looking me in the eye. I asked Reverend Choy for a replacement, but he keeps sending Pioneer. I suspect he wants to compromise me, blackmail me. But how? I have no wife to betray, I have no reputation to defend. The only danger I foresee is if Reverend Choy tells Pioneer's husband, Dealer Dong Dong, that I tried to molest her. Or offered her money to rub my loins. For safety's sake, I spend most of the day on the open veranda for all to see. I did think of passing my time in Quack Du Fu's shop, but he will talk of you and Ma Hongniang and this will pain me, so I keep my own miserable company.

★

Harris knocked weakly on my door. As soon as I opened it and saw his face, I knew you were lost to me, lost from me, dear Sweet Li Jie. But then I checked and chided myself. Perhaps, I thought, you were alive, back home, guarded by Wang Changling and Baoyu. Perhaps Quack Du Fu was wrong and you never set off for Demerara; you are still in The Domain of Wang Qian where I left

141

you. Yes, let me believe that, let me book passage and come to you.

There had been a drowning, a boatload of Chinese travelling the river had capsized. He had got this much from the Carib bush people. "They had found the boat, but no bodies," Harris said. "A few things washed up on the shore: clothes, bags with Chinese foodstuffs, but no bodies. The alligators would have eaten all of the people."

I wish he had not divulged this last detail.

★

Dear Sweet Li Jie, today I took up paper and wrote in my best English to make it sound formal and final, giving permission to Harris to dispose of all my goods in Gladstone Town. He is empowered to gather as many cloth merchants and tailors as he could to my shop and to sell everything. I knew my belongings by heart, every single needle, scissors, ruler. I set out the price of everything, calculated what monies would be made after a hefty discount to buyers and gave the inventory to Harris. I spent time hunched over the paper, listing goods, inserting figures to distract me from dwelling on you. I failed. Working with numbers once gave me some kind of solace, but no more. Each item I penned, each scratch the nib made on paper, brought your cries to my ears. Did you call out my name at the end? And why did you not seek me out when you arrived in Demerara? Why venture upriver, risk its rapids, its veiled currents? But, let me pause, let me not imagine…

★

Dear Sweet Li Jie, Harris will return from Gladstone Town in one month's time, by my reckoning. I have departed Prospect and I am now in Georgetown City, awaiting a ship to return me home. The sea is blown into fury, so I will wait for calmness to return to make a safe passage back to you. I will settle in your village and propose marriage. I will have to put up with Landlord Wang Changling, his unruly behaviour to his tenants and his high rents. But I must not judge him harshly. I hear he has been uncommonly kind to you and Ma Hongniang. I am staying again with Glutton Fu. On hearing of my coming, he spruced up my old room, though the tinsel which he stretched along one wall only mocked me with its glitter.

I try not to go outside the hotel since the sight of bicycles only makes me accuse myself of bringing possible disaster to you, and the constant ringing of bells maddens me. I stay in the near darkness of my room; the other occupants avoid me. Learning of my loss, they fear I will bring bad luck onto them. Only Glutton Fu comes to see me with plates of food or to refill the oil lamp. He speaks of his sorrow for me. Tears come to his eyes, he lowers his head. He has been doing so for a week now, muttering the same words. I asked him to stop speaking to me and just serve me food and deal with my laundry and refill my oil-lamp. I was sure his show of sympathy was exactly that: a show calculated to open my purse to him. I prefer silence and near-darkness to best remember your face and your ways. I seize upon memories of your small actions, simple gestures. Like when you were with Landlord Wang Changling at the bookshop eating oranges. Not sucking loudly, not spitting out the seeds in the normal vulgar way, but raising your hand to your mouth to gather them and Baoyu taking them from you. If I told Glutton Fu this, or anyone else, he would think me mad and stupid. But in all the months I've spent in Demerara, when I have thought of my Master, Yu Hao, who perished on the ship, what always comes to mind are the small, common things like the way he polished his spectacles, the way he placed his pencil behind his ear, the way he held a tea cup with both hands, the way he cracked his knuckles before turning to the ledger books (a habit which I have taken on), the way he rubbed his eyes at the end of the day out of tiredness, not with fingers but the palm of each hand. I don't hear his words, I can't mimic the sound of his voice, so the very things that made him a man are lost – except his ordinary gestures which lodge and will not budge from my mind.

★

To draw me out of my lonely isolation, Glutton Fu insisted I go with him to some fortune tellers.

"True and wise Chinese, I trust them. At least two of them said that by year-end I would have to build a new floor for my hotel, because plenty more ships will come from China, plenty more people looking for lodgings. I have already got a new wagon, a longer wagon to fetch their goods."

It was the very same Black Duck who had taken me to Gladstone Town more than a year before, and helped me arrange my dwelling, who now took Glutton Fu and me to a small cluster of houses – more huts than houses – at the far corner of Georgetown, where two dozen or so Chinese squatted. As the horse struggled through a mud dam to reach them, I thought of my faithful donkey who, burdened with cloth, had taken me without complaint to the villages. When my business was over, I would instruct Harris to give the animal to Gurr who would find some good use for it. The villagers trudged miles in the hot sun to visit the one doctor in Gladstone Town, so the donkey and cart could be their ambulance.

It was shocking to see the Chinese squatting area. Huts without doors, windows roofed with rotting branches. The canal beside which they lived was their mainstay. It contained only a few fish, though crabs were everywhere. The trees lining its banks provided firewood.

"I help them out a lot," Glutton Fu said when he saw the dismay in my eyes. "But you can only do so much…"

"How do you help them out?" I asked, looking at the bony, barefooted men casting nets into the water and drawing in one or two fish. Years of living off the canal had depleted the stock. "They will manage," Glutton Fu said. "Some fish breed quicker and grow fatter than others, so folk let the fish alone for a few weeks to give them space and licence."

I was no more impressed by Glutton Fu's wisdom about fish than I had been by Harris's.

"How do you help them?" I asked a second time.

He clamped his lips together, not wanting to speak. Only when I glared at him did he say in a halting way, in a voice tinged with shame, that he ferried many of his hotel guests to the fortune tellers.

"As soon as the ship lands, they come to me. They are full of questions, full of worry. So I bring them here to find out their future."

"The fortune-tellers obviously didn't read their own palms, otherwise they would not have set foot in Demerara to live in such a pit," I said.

144

Glutton Fu fell silent. Then before I could question him again, he went off to fetch two prophets.

Waggoner Black Duck leant close towards me and whispered, "It's all a scam. He talks to all his guests, gets to know the details of their lives, then he passes this information on to the fortune tellers who know exactly what to say when they meet the people he has sent. He gets half the money paid."

"I suspected this," I said. "I know another Chinese who cheats those in his care. A Christian pastor at that."

"Everybody in the Colony is a thief; every race is thieving from the others and among themselves," Waggoner Black Duck said. "Even Fu's own brother thiefed from him. Fu lent money to his brother, Longping, to open a gambling den close to the house he bought in Gladstone – the one you rent. His brother made a little fortune but spent it out on opium and whores. Fu didn't see a penny back!"

Poor Harris… His Speck had flicked in the water and grown up to be a human crook. Even so, I agreed to listen to the fortune tellers. One had blackened teeth and protruding bones, the other a belly swollen with malnutrition and a scar above one of his eyebrows, no doubt the result of some squabble over scraps. I could have just given them some money and made my way back to the hotel, but I stayed to show them respect, a show lost on them, having been treated in the Colony for so long as cane-trash. One told me, having looked over my ears, head, and eyebrows, that I was 'wood and water', a happy combination which meant years of prosperous dealings. The other shook a bamboo cylinder until an incense stick came out, a Chinese character inked on it. I doubted whether he could read it.

He stared at it, then spoke to me in broken language, taking up the previous revelation. "I see a vessel, wood and water, a riverboat, wood and water, everyone is safe, they paddle happily."

I raised my hand to hit him but pity froze it – and my overwhelming desire to believe him. I gave him and the other man double the sum agreed and more, enough to pay their dues to Glutton Fu and still eat for the day.

★

"They found nobody on the riverbank," Glutton Fu said. "So you can't know that Sweet Li Jie is drowned. And why trust a quack like Du Fu or some bush savages saying a boat capsized? Boats overturn all the time – hidden rocks in the water or big, big trees crashing down, the wind toppling them. The newspapers didn't name anybody. It only reported the story because they were Chinese people. I never hear Chinese people drown before. It would be a first. It was news for a day. The river continues to flow; Coolies and Negroes continue to drown; everybody continues buying and selling."

I didn't bother to raise my hand to him or even try to stop his ramble. All I could think about was boarding the ship back to China. The *James Moses* had arrived a week ago and after repairs and restocking, would set sail a week hence. A long journey. Harris had told me about the invention of the airship; I wished there was one here to whisk me to you.

★

Dear Sweet Li Jie, I am waiting in Georgetown and writing to you in the certainty (which dwindles to a hope, then swells to a certainty again, then recedes to a hope) that you and Ma Hongniang are alive and in Wang Changling's care, that you never left China in the first place. I write all manner of nonsense, bits of people's conversations, the colour of rain, and more. But I'm done now. I will only tell you quickly about my parting with Harris and Gurr, then I will board ship and come to you.

Harris returned from Albion with a bag full of money and my trunk in which he had placed some of my clothes and the painted vase with your picture on it, carefully wrapped in a length of cloth to protect it against damage.

"Take half the money," I said, not bothering to count, holding up the vase to the light to admire Gurr's restoration.

"I don't want money. I don't live by money," Harris said.

"You and your wisdom about trees, shrubs, fish, bush animals! You can't eat wisdom. You can't buy and sell with it. It has no currency."

I instantly regretted mocking what was otherworldly and mysterious about him, but his slippers were ragged and his clothes needed renewal.

"Give your half then to Gurr. Tell him to buy plasters and

ointments. Children are always climbing and falling out of fruit trees. He can be the village dispenser. Remove all the Chinese medicines I have in the trunk. Give them to him. All the jars are labelled. He'll know what to use. Tell him I'm giving him money in memory of my friend, Dr Richmond."

Reluctantly, Harris took a handful of coins, to appease me.

In truth, in my solitude in Glutton Fu's hotel, Master Yu Hao came to mind again and again. I thought of all the nastiness I had endured: mosquitoes, gnats, the blistering heat, cheating humans... But as soon as Master Yu Hao appeared in my daydream, his kindness banished all thoughts of cruelty.

Harris wanted to stay with me until it was time to board the ship, but I sent him away with gentle words.

He knew by his peculiar instinct that I needed solitude to dwell on you, Sweet Li Jie, to be excited by the prospect of meeting you and Ma Hongniang in your hamlet. I wanted to believe the fortune-tellers, and Harris sensed my desperation. He left without complaint. As he hugged me, he whispered words which I suppose he had rehearsed for a moment like this.

"How small we are, Mr Jia Yun, and yet, how big!"

Eleven of the simplest words that a child might utter. I was expecting something more grand and memorable. He sensed my dismay and continued: "Things are the same though we are no more."

Oh Harris! Oh glittering speck! What will become of him, I wondered, all that day and all of my remaining hours in Demerara.

★

Dear Sweet Li Ji, on the day of boarding, Glutton Fu came to my room in a state of excitement, showing me the *Demerara Chronicle*. The timing was so coincidental that for a moment I thought the gods had conspired to make my parting from Demerara bearable.

"My goodbye gift to you," Glutton Fu said, pressing the newspaper into my hand. He beamed. "I am happy for you that you didn't invest!"

It was a front page article on the death of Reverend Choy. He had absconded from Prospect Town with all the church's money. He had taken Pioneer with him. She deserted her husband,

Dealer Dong Dong, taking his stock of gold. Prospect Town was in disarray. Many were destitute since they had given money to Reverend Choy to pay their rent, a year in advance, to Church headquarters in Georgetown. The Church was repossessing their properties and seeking other tenants. They petitioned the Bishop in Georgetown who said the matter was in the hands of God, since the Church, too, had invested large sums in Prospect Town and was itself facing bankruptcy. The police had found Reverend Choy and Pioneer sheltering in a Carib village upriver. He fired at them. They fired back and both fugitives were killed. Just like that! The story of Prospect, its goals, its efforts, its dreams ended, just like that! I had feared, when I first set sight on Prospect, that the project would collapse, as the ocelot did, but I suspected it would take years before the jungle took over.

Their bodies were paddled back to Georgetown but had rotted during the long journey. The police threw the bodies into a ditch for dogs to devour. The Bishop condemned the police for their unchristian behaviour and accused them, being black, of bias against the Chinese. The Bishop feared that people would use the Prospect Town disaster to vent their anger at the Chinese, loot a few shops, burn down some houses, even though such rioters had no business whatever with Prospect Town. Any excuse to make havoc and thieve, the Bishop thundered.

"He is a white man, he has no time for Congoes," Glutton Fu said.

No doubt the newspaper would carry tales of Prospect for months to come, but I didn't want to know.

It was time to flee the colony! My month-end had come. I set off now to find you in the *flesh*, in matter.

148

PART SIX

CHAPTER 1
The end of ink

Wang Changling sat at his desk beside an open window to catch the breeze. It was an unusually hot day. He was in the midst of pleasing thoughts. Ma Hongniang and Sweet Li Jie had brought such happiness to his household. In moments like these he couldn't help recalling his creation, Ying Ying, and, nervously, reluctantly, he put his freshly carved pen to paper, knowing that the first word he wrote would lead to others, unleashing fantasies that he had suppressed since Ma Hongniang and Sweet Li Jie had appeared at his door. So why did he take up his pen, why did he break his resolve? If asked, he couldn't have explained it, what spell had been cast upon him and made him a serf to ink. Explanation meant reason and reason meant hope, but there was no reason, no hope in what he was doing. He was just doing.

A sentence suggested itself. He watched his hand making marks on the paper as if it did not belong to him, as if it had a will of its own which could not be restrained. He raised his head from the desk, sighed deeply. It was the last sound he made before a bullet pierced his forehead, leaving scraps of bone and gore on the ground. Blood trickled down his neck. Wang Changling thought it was sweat – it was an unusually hot day – then his mind went blank.

★

Baoyu, who was poised to bite into a corn cob, was left with his mouth open. He clutched the edge of the table for support. It was Ma Hongniang who, with a strength that surprised her, hoisted him from the chair and practically lifted him to the door, past the slumped body of Wang Changling, kicking aside the hens who had wandered into the house out of curiosity. The noise of the gunshot had not scattered them. Odd, Ma Hongniang thought, her mind dwelling on the behaviour of the hens rather than on the bullet that had blown away bits of Wang Changling's brain. Sweet Li Jie, who was in the yard playing with coloured pebbles, rushed to the window where she saw Wang Changling's body kowtowing towards on the table, his head resting on it as if in prayer and worship of his ancestors. Without needing to be told, she quietly followed her mother and Baoyu across the field to their hiding place in the hills. On his shopping journeys to town, Wang Changling had heard that soldiers were apparently approaching from the South, though no one knew whether they were bandits or British. Wang Changling had dismissed this news as gossip: how often had he been warned about invaders and warlords but none had come. He had decided not to fortify his house with weaponry nor to instruct his serfs to guard its perimeter. Still, out of concern for Ma Hongniang and Sweet Li Jie, he had stocked a cave in the hills with gourds of water, dried fruit, smoked meats, cotties of rice, enough food to survive for a week or two, plus money and jewellery, which could easily secure their passage out of the province to a place of safety. Baoyu would be their bodyguard if they needed to escape. Ever since Ma Hongniang and Sweet Li Jie had appeared at his door, Wang Changling's sole concern had been their welfare. They had long ceased being strangers but were treated fiercely, as family.

Two years of uneventful happiness had passed in Wang Changling's household. Ma Hongniang had made good her skills in baking cakes but also in creating pottery to appease the gods, buried in the earth to encourage harvests, to increase the breeding of goats and pigs. In this way, she increased the number of hens, so not only was the household supplied with fresh eggs, but every few months she sacrificed the fattest one to the gods, its beak buried at the edge of the village pond to pluck rain from the sky and fill it.

At first Wang Changling had been excited to take Sweet Li Jie to market to buy books and he had begun to teach her to read, but the stories were all about blood-letting so he desisted, knowing this would remind her of the murder of her father. In any case, Sweet Li Jie was artistic; she loved moulding clay and grinding stones to make dyes for her mother. And riding her bicycle to the market with baskets of plums. When they had first arrived, Ma Hongniang had been reluctant to live under Wang Changling's roof. She wanted to avoid gossip, but also to be faithful to the memory of her husband. She and Sweet Li Jie moved out of Wang Changling's house after a week, and they lived a bare existence in a small bamboo cottage for half a year, refusing any more food or clothing from Wang Changling, and even paying rent. It was only when her husband entered her dream, not once but four times, instructing her to partake of Wang Changling's hospitality for the sake of Sweet Li Jie's safety, that she relented. In the last dream, he held up the hatchet with which the foreign devil had chopped his throat, to warn her of the need to protect the child. The blade caught the sunlight and flashed into her eyes. She awoke with a lurch and Sweet Li Jie stirred from her sleep and began to cry for no reason, perhaps sensing the terror in Ma Hongniang's mind.

Even when there was no longer any need for Sweet Li Jie to go to the market with plums, she did it out of habit. After a while, the sheer excitement of cycling, of manoeuvring around puddles or rocks, or turning corners without toppling (each basket carefully weighed and balanced on the handlebars) had changed her character. She smiled to herself when she reached the market with not a single plum lost. She smiled to herself when she made a good sale. Outwardly, though, she was as glum as ever, not wanting to expose her gladness to strangers.

★

Only Baoyu seemed to draw some reaction from her. At first, Ma Hongniang was suspicious of a grown man like Baoyu playing with her daughter. Maybe his intent was as ugly as his appearance. He made her special soups from bamboo shoots, not the common onion broth he served Wang Changling. He made her porridge with fruits he mashed together to create secret flavours, which only they shared, and she let him spoon it directly into her mouth. He fashioned whistles from pieces of bamboo, he built her a birdcage, stilts and other creations to amuse her. She was fascinated by the use of his circus knife, mesmerised by his skilful hands. She let him use his knife to cut her hair, and he held the blade sideways so she could see her reflection and be contented.

They spent many hours alone, and far from home, gathering unusual herbs for Ma Hongniang's pot. She reluctantly put aside her anxiety, but would remain vigilant. Quack Du Fu's concoction to cure Sweet Li Jie of depression hadn't worked; Baoyu could hardly do worse in trying to lighten her mood. Besides which, Baoyu was a better barber than she was!

★

After they had settled in the household, Wang Changling decided to give up writing forever and to satisfy himself by being their protector. Ma Hongniang resembled his own mother. He was unsure about this to begin with, since the image of his mother had faded in his mind, but as time passed he began to accept that Ma Hongniang resembled her, and that, like his mother, she could play the lute. This brought tears of happiness to Wang Changling. He had gifted the lute to her and was amazed at how quickly she learnt to play it. He believed that it was his mother's spirit guiding her fingers (when in fact it was Ma Hongniang's subtlety in shaping clay which she transferred to the strings). As for Sweet Li Jie, she had taken the place of Ying Ying in his mind – Ying Ying, the first maiden character he had created when he composed his first story. He had imagined himself as the figure of the Emperor about to order the execution of the rebel Yang Lun, when Ying Ying, his favourite concubine, appeared. He remembered how he had described her oval face, her eyebrows joined, her almond-shaped eyes, how she wore hair clasps in the form of phoenixes facing the sun, the gleam of which blinded him. He had been enfeebled by her loveliness. Now that Ying Ying had become Sweet Li Jie, he had been freed from having to dream of her in writing, though Sweet Li Jie became his daughter, not his lover. He had decided to purge himself of base desire by ridding himself of pages, paper, pen. From the time of his first story, Ying Ying had been lodged in his mind, but he could not confess this to anyone, even to his mother if she'd been alive.

★

It was Ma Hongniang who had broached the subject of marriage. Wang Changling had decided never to ask her about her husband or other family matters. The nature of their relationship would mark a fresh start to his life. He had long before removed his books from the study to make space for mother and daughter's bed. The bookshelf now housed their clothing. Baoyu had already burned or buried all his master's writing (except for a few pages, which he'd hidden under a large flat stone in the far end of the barn, thinking one day to offer it to the bookseller for a few yuans, in case the story the pages told was any good). Coincidentally, when Baoyu and Sweet Li Jie had gone off to a far corner of the pasture and were digging a grave for Wang Changling's scribblings, they had unearthed a belt hook with a frog-clasp, thumb rings and brooches which bore all the signs of being ancient. Wang Changling was overjoyed. He deemed the discovery a sign that the gods were intent on showering blessings on the new household. He gladly gave the treasure to mother and child.

Ma Hongniang, presenting him dumplings for his lunch, put the question to him in a casual way, as if it was of no consequence, an idle thought. "Why did you never take a wife?" she asked. The question unsettled him, she sensed his discomfort and made amends by buttering slices of bread to go with the dumplings. Fortunately Baoyu and Sweet Li Jie returned from picking mushrooms. Ma Hongniang hurried back to the kitchen to prepare food for them.

"Yes, I am a man of wealth and many women would be drawn to me, but my mother is not here to choose for me," Wang Changling had thought, dwelling on Ma Hongniang's question and coming up with very few explanations as to his unwed state, and these, even to him, were hollow. But how could he confess his absorption with Ying Ying whom he had created in his very first story? None of the women whom he met on his visits to nearby towns could match Ying Ying's elegance, her almond-shaped eyes sparkling with a world of feeling, and as bright as autumn ripples. Not even his mother bore Ying Ying's beauty. It was only someone as richly imagined as Ying Ying he would marry. When he created her, in a few movements of his pen, he had been dumbstruck by the mysterious workings of his mind, and began to distrust himself. Still, he wished Ying Ying would somehow reveal herself not in dream but in actual *flesh*. His frustration was constant. He'd spend dozens of lines trying to describe her more fully, and to court her, to conjure her to his marriage bed. "I belong to a place where willows flourish," she said, denying him, disappearing from his dreams for many days before returning. Appearing and withdrawing, Ying Ying was a constant torment. He was elated when Ma Hongniang and Sweet Li Jie arrived, he knew right away they would be a real comfort to his loneliness and distract him from his obsession with Ying Ying, if not cure him of it. With them in his household, his frustration gave way to a gratitude that Ying Ying would remain always in an unreality which could never age her, sicken her, bond her to the corruption of flesh. Let her remain beyond ink. Instead, he would find satisfaction in companionship with Ma Hongniang and Sweet Li Ji, his new family whom the gods had guided to his door as compensation.

Of course, he could never answer Ma Hongniang's question about marriage by disclosing his love for Ying Ying. She would rightly laugh at his foolishness. He himself was aware of his defect but he could control Ying Ying even less than he could manage his serfs. She came and went from his mind at her own will, no General, no Emperor could command her.

★

Having removed Baoyu to the safety of the cave, Ma Hongniang hoped his howling would stop, but he would not be consoled. He called out Swallow Tail's name. He had divulged to Ma Hongniang his longing for Swallow Tail and his terror that he might never see her again. The circus moved to different provinces and would be near-impossible to trace. His howling now came from panic; Swallow Tail was surely lost, because the murder of Wang Changling meant he would never have the wherewithal to journey in search of her.

Unlike Baoyu, who remained steadfast in his memory of Swallow Tail, Ma Hongniang had eventually blotted out her husband from her mind. During the years in Wang Changling's household she had focused on Sweet Li Jie's welfare. In any case, her husband had been somewhat of a stranger, spending months apart from her, since he travelled from town to town, selling kitchenware, ladles and the like. He was always exhausted and short of money when he came home, so she had begun to suspect that he had mistresses in various towns. As to Sweet Li Jie, Baoyu had become her idol, entertainer and father-like protector. They spent days foraging for wild berries and Baoyu would spend hours telling her about his time in the circus and teaching her the art of knife-throwing. Wang Changling's murder revived her memory of her father, and with Baoyu's own distress, once more Sweet Li Jie withdrew into herself, hiding in the farthest space of the cave.

They spent two weeks waiting for soldiers to arrive, the rash of war having spread all over the country, even reaching their humble village. But when they came there were only a handful of foreign devils, and though they came to ransack the houses, there was not much to take and in any case the villagers had buried whatever was precious to them. So, instead of shovelling here and there to unearth what was buried, they just moved on to richer plunder elsewhere.

Ma Hongniang gathered Sweet Li Jie, Baoyu and a few villagers, with whatever wealth they had. They journeyed by foot, at night, to the port where ships set sail for Demerara. She remembered Suitor Jia Yun telling her of his impending voyage and the prospect of wealth, and the many happy Chinese settlements in the new land. They would journey there, outwait the skirmishes and killings in the province, all the while gathering goods in Demerara, land of gold, and when the time came, and warfare ended, they would return with glitter and sackfuls.

★

Wang Changling had taken up his pen for the first time for countless months. He would bid farewell to Ying Ying forever. He was reluctant to address her, and felt he was being ungrateful to the gods who had delivered Ma Hongniang and Sweet Li Jie to him. He was reluctant to disobey the gods, but Ying Ying still forced herself into his mind. He could not resist her almond eyes, her blossom-white skin, her dulcet voice calling to him from an unknown place. It was whilst poised over a sheet of paper, ink gathering at the bamboo tip, that he mused momentarily on whether writing to Ying Ying was an act of sinning, even though his letter would be suffused with love. Why should writing about the love that survives farewell be sinful? He would no longer cherish the memory of her being, he would no longer crave her presence. Forever absent, no longer being Ying Ying… This was his final thought before the gunshot dropped him, a piece of his brain flicked to the desk, another piece flicked to the ground, and ants gathered to take the news to his mother.

EPILOGUE

Baoyu had been disloyal. Instead of burning Wang Changling's writings, he had secreted a few pages in his pants. As soon as Wang Changling had left the hamlet on some business or other, Baoyu saddled a horse and pelted across the fields to the market and the bookseller. He would sell the pages, but not keep the money for himself. Instead, he would buy Sweet Li Jie a dress, as a suitor would, from the cloth shop nearby. For years he had been affected by the story Ma Hongniang told about how, when they were escaping from the devils who killed her husband, they ate pieces of Sweet Li Jie's dress out of hunger. He would haggle with the proprietor and his young apprentice, having seen how they surrendered to people begging, holding up their pitiful children. On his many visits to the bookseller, with Wang Changling and Sweet Li Jie, he would look mournfully at the cloth shop, knowing he had no money to buy her a gift. It would be his way of paying tribute to Swallow Tail. In all his years in the circus, the most he had given Swallow Tail was fruit fallen on the ground, the ants brushed off, the skin wiped clean. A gift to Sweet Li Jie might still his anguish at losing Swallow Tail.

The bookseller took what seemed like hours to read Baoyu's offering. He read and reread. Baoyu wanted to hurry home, before Wang Changling returned. At last the bookseller looked up at Baoyu and said: "This is not for me. It will not fetch a yuan." He gestured to the books stacked on his shelves. "All about rebellions, all about the most powerful Emperors, all about blood-letting, concubines, rape, starvation. Nowadays people want a misty love story, people want a perfumed garden."

Baoyu didn't understand what the bookseller was saying.

"And it's badly done, in fact it's foul, the work of a hopeless

159

scribbler." As soon as he spoke, the bookseller bunched his hand as if to cuff himself. He suddenly realised that the writing was possibly done by Wang Changling, who might have asked Baoyu to present it for an assessment of its merit. Baoyu had told the bookseller that the pages were loose leaves in a book which Wang Changling had read and put away. When he had been dusting the library, the loose leaves floated to the ground, to his feet, as if the book was bestowing him with a gift from its bosom. Her bosom, the book must be a female. Why else would Wang Changling devote so much time to it, licking his lips as he read?

What to do, the bookseller asked himself, regretting that he had insulted Wang Changling, his best and most lavish customer! Baoyu looked as stupid as ever, but the bookseller couldn't take the chance that Baoyu was not genuinely dull. "I was only trying to beat down the price," he told Baoyu. "Truth is, the story of the Yang Lun Rebellion is… Never mind, bring me more pages, and more pages, if your Master allows." He gave Baoyu an excessive sum, taking the pages between thumb and forefinger, as if handling a soiled napkin or a silken, delicately sequined piece of embroidery.

The Yang Lun Rebellion

The Emperor was facing a fierce rebellion by Yang Lun, formerly a field-hand and gardener. Ungrateful wretch! He had promoted Yang Lun, treated him as a son. He had given Yang Lun a title, made him his confidante and junior counsellor, with quarters at Court furnished with sandalwood tables; walls hung with scroll-pictures of dragons riding waves; lacquered carriages draped with the finest curtains. His own barbers attended to Yang Lun, plaiting his hair with silk, and braiding it in expensive oils. His own tailors dressed Yang Lun in satin trousers, brocaded stockings. Yang Lun spent his youth at cock fights and pleasure trips, seeming to luxuriate in idleness, but all the time he was plotting the day when he would topple the Emperor. Why? Starved in a dungeon for a week and beaten with iron chains, Yang Lun still could not explain why he had incited rebellion, knowing that he would fail since he could only muster two hundred men to his

side. His rebels were untrained in arms. They were malnour-
ished, mainly elderly. They joined out of desperation, for a few
coins and Yang Lun's promise that, afterwards, they could ransack the Emperor's palace and cart off its treasures and concubines. They began by storming the palace walls but were stopped
in a hail of arrows. They were all slain within the hour, apart from
Yang Lun and two servants who managed to escape to the woods
but were quickly found. The two servants were hacked to pieces
and fed to hogs; Yang Lun was bundled into the dungeon to be
beaten with iron chains. Why, the Emperor demanded, as Yang
Lun was tied to the chopping block, but Yang Lun was mute. His
jaw had been broken, his head dented, lice fed on his dried blood.
His side-locks, once daintily looped, were tousled like
tumbleweeds. Perhaps he was too damaged to speak, his mind
deranged by the beatings. The Emperor suddenly felt a surge of
pity within, unexpected because it was rare. The only time he had
felt such emotion was as a boy when all his songbirds died in their
cages for no apparent reason. He had woken up, bathed, dressed
and, as was his habit, rushed to his birds to feed them even before
his own repast. The curtains were lifted from the cages. An
unspeakable scene! Feathers stiff, the crimson and blue already
fading. He was numb for days. It was only when his guardian-
uncle, to appease him, ordered the live burial of all the keepers of
birds and their wives and children in the palace grounds, that the
boy Emperor regained some speech. New birds were presented
to him but he cared little for them, for when they sang, all he
could hear was the whimpering of the keepers as they were being
thrown into the burial pit with their families.

The Emperor rose from his throne to command the sword to
fall on Yang Lun, but his Favourite Concubine stopped his hand
and placed it to her bosom. He gazed upon her oval face, her
almond-shaped eyes. He was enfeebled by her loveliness. She
wore hair-clasps in the form of phoenixes facing the sun, the
gleam of which blinded him.

"I have been in a place where willows flourish," she said, her
eyes sparkling with a world of feeling. And before he could
respond, she said, "I went there to meditate, now I have returned
to save you from the desolation of your doing." She turned to

address the throng of courtiers and ladies in the same seductive voice, her eyes still as bright as autumn ripples, not a sign of contempt on her face. "You ladies in tiaras set in pearls, turquoise capes, jade pendants tinkling as you approach; you men in silks, in swords, in golden ornaments... You are of such glory that the world rarely sees. Your worthy deeds, your command of people, your valour, are celebrated in all corners of the earth. Your wisdom is distilled from the teachings of a hundred generations. Why, then, do you stay silent whilst your Emperor behaves like a churl? Yes, a churl, for why else would he ordain the torture and beheading of Yang Lun, the one he loves?"

The gathering was stunned, then a murmur arose which swelled into a rush of noise. They looked to the Emperor for guidance, but he raised his hand, banished all but his bodyguards from his presence. He needed to be alone with his Favourite Concubine, to learn from her the mystery of his ways.

"Remember Yang Lun's handsomeness, when you first caught sight of him? You were looking out of a window, sipping tea, still mourning for your songbirds years after they had died. Yang Lun walked past, at a distance, bearing garden shears. Even though two bow-shots afar, you were struck by the gracefulness with which he leant over the flower beds, the way sunlight reflected off his naked arms, the care with which he plucked dead flowers to allow the living to thrive. Your tea grew tepid, then tastelessly cold. All morning you watched him attending to the orchids with devotion, even adoration. Courtiers came with urgent affairs of state but you dismissed them, entranced by the youth moving gently between rows of flowers, stooping to take in their scent. You summoned Yang Lun to your presence. Your heart quickened as the youth entered. His fingers were stained with sap. He smelled of cinnamon. Although poorly dressed, you sensed a certain dignity which Yang Lun wore effortlessly. So nervous were you that you had to clear your throat twice before you could pronounce Yang Lun the new keeper of the plants in your private rooms."

Favourite Concubine reminded the Emperor that he was then twenty-two, some seven years older than Yang Lun whom he quickly adopted as a playmate, making personal choice of his new attire, supervising the dressing of his hair, the rubbing of rare oils into his skin to arouse his blood to liveliness. He had seated Yang Lun on his lap and made him run his fingers through his beard, and even pluck it to make him start. "My little panda," the Emperor had said, stroking his face to the amusement of the Court.

"You pampered him," Favourite Concubine scolded. "You made him so neglectful of his duties that the plants wilted and even stank since you would not allow their removal. All he lived for was his garden; he had flowers, he was not in want. But you spoilt him." The Emperor lowered his eyes as she recalled an unfortunate concubine who took it upon herself to remove the most rotten plant, and was ordered to be taken to the nearest cliff and thrown to her death. Another, merely smiling at Yang Lun, provoked the Emperor's rage and she suffered the same fate. Before the year was out, a dozen others, who did nothing more than glance at the youth, or touch their lips in his presence or, out of nervousness, stumbled slightly as he passed by, were taken to the spot renamed *The Concubines' Flight Before The Winds of Wrath*. They begged to be strangled instead of being hurled over the ravine, but the Emperor would not relent.

"Enough of killing! They were my companions. My eunuch would have given them a potion, then strangled them in their sleep. But you were base and bloodthirsty. Think upon your vile deeds!"

The Emperor didn't immediately remember the keepers of his song birds, nor the dozens sacrificed at the *Concubines' Flight Before The Winds of Wrath*. He did not remember the servant who fed him soup but let slip a drop upon his garment. He was boiled alive, then fed to his own family.

There were others, but when Favourite Concubine awakened his memory, it was only the Eunuch-from-Xian he recalled instantly. There were many eunuchs at his service, but the Eunuch-from-Xian was their master, being the eldest and most favoured. His fellow eunuchs had to carry around their necks jars of brine containing their severed testicles, but he was exempt from this humiliation. When the Emperor was a young boy of ten, the Eunuch-from-Xian would sit him in his lap, stroke his hair, and whisper into his ear. He loved the Eunuch-from-Xian's caress or sudden tickling or playful pinching. The Eunuch-from-Xian's hands strayed frequently along the boy-Emperor's thighs, and the boy-Emperor sighed. The other eunuchs grew jealous, they reported the Eunuch-from-Xian to the Emperor's guardian-uncle. He was executed after due torture, for the duration of a full moon, and within earshot of the boy-Emperor, to purge him of any longing for the forbidden.

The boy-Emperor grieved but could do nothing to prevent the secateurs and the clippers being applied to the Eunuch-from-Xian's body. He was a willowy man, but when they had done with him he was a cactus.

Years later, the Emperor made Yang Lun put aside such garden implements and sit on his lap, cuddling him, cooing into his ears like a turtle dove, but Yang Lun never relaxed as the boy-Emperor had done in the Eunuch-from-Xian's lap. He surrendered, to be sure, but the Emperor sensed that within he was wriggling to be free. When Yang Lun grew older, he was bold enough to stop the Emperor's hand.

Yang Lun sought every occasion to escape the Court, to cockfights and on pleasure trips, but the Emperor always sent soldiers to retrieve him. Once he absconded with a few of his old gardening tools and hid in the woods. His joy at being once more in the company of flowers and berries was soon ended, because the Emperor had spies everywhere. It was the quietest of spots, with no humans for miles around, so Yang Lun was at a loss to understand how he had been betrayed and taken back to the Emperor's bed. Perhaps the Emperor was supreme over fowl and fish and everything that moved over the earth, as everyone believed. He, too, had believed this, at first, until he felt the Emperor's nose rooting at his flesh or heard his snoring – deeds unbecoming of a divine ruler. But perhaps it was true, perhaps a butterfly or a ladybird spotted him in the woods and reported it to the Emperor.

"Enough of killing," Favourite Concubine urged, and the Emperor relented, and began to sob in front of his bodyguards.

"I missed him so much!" he cried. "I wanted him back. I sent battalions of my best soldiers to find him when he absconded…"

Favourite Concubine held the Emperor's head in her hands and soaked up his tears in her handkerchief, as he confessed to her that even when news reached him that Yang Lun was preparing a rebellion, he, the Emperor, remained steadfast in his affection for Yang Lun.

"If I be overthrown by a rival, let it be by Yang Lun. Let me die by Yang Lun's graceful hand and not by some low-bred sullen subordinate," he said. The Emperor recalled the day when Yang Lun's rebellion was crushed and Yang Lun brought before him in chains. "I went to embrace him but he would not acknowledge my sorrow. He shunned my outstretched hand. He turned his back to me and laughed. I commanded him to face me, but when he did so it was only to spit at my feet and called me a..."

The Emperor could not bring himself to utter the word. He slouched in his throne, a picture of helplessness and shame.

"Stay with me, don't abandon me, teach me what it is to long for a woman as I did for you in our first days," the Emperor pleaded with Favourite Concubine, claiming that he only wanted Yang Lun tortured to rid him of his wildness, to convert him into a slave creature like his songbirds. They closed their eyes and cooed when he stroked their feathers, then in utmost repose they surrendered themselves into the palm of his hand. Even when the cage doors were left open, they would not seek freedom.

ABOUT THE AUTHOR

David Dabydeen was born on a sugar estate in Berbice, Guyana in 1956. His family lived for a time in New Amsterdam where he attended school. At the age of around ten he won a scholarship to Queen's College in Georgetown where he studied for a couple of years. He gained a place at Cambridge University in 1974 and read English there and at London Universities, completing his doctorate in 1982. He was a post-doctoral fellow at Oxford University for three years. He is currently Emeritus Professor at the University of Warwick and was for some years Guyana's Ambassador in China.

His poetry includes *Slave Song* winner of the Quiller-Couch prize and the Commonwealth Poetry Prize; *Coolie Odyssey* (1988) and *Turner – New and Selected Poetry* (1994), and republished by Peepal Tree in 2002.

His novels include *The Intended* (1991), *Disappearance* (1993), *The Counting House* (1996), *A Harlot's Progress* (1999), *Our Lady of Demerara* (2004, 2008), *Molly and the Muslim Stick* (2008), and *Johnson's Dictionary* (2013).

In addition to his fiction and poetry, David Dabydeen has written two works of art history, *Hogarth's Blacks: Images of Blacks in Eighteenth Century English Art* (1987) and *Hogarth, Walpole and Commercial Britain* (1987) and a critical work, *A Reader's Guide to West Indian and Black British Literature* (1988). He is the editor of *The Black Presence in English Literature* (1985); *India in the Caribbean* (1987); *A Handbook for Teaching Caribbean Literature* (1988); *Black Writers in Britain, 1760-1890* (1991); *Across the Dark Waters: Indian Identity in the Caribbean* (1996).